"...
to
Have..., ...

He gave her a mocking smile.

She flushed and glanced down at her hands clenched tightly in front of her, as if to create a barrier between them.

He tipped up her chin. "Do you think you can reform a rake like me?"

She licked her lips before answering. "Do you need reforming?" She found her gaze drawn to his mouth, just inches above hers. She caught her breath at the thought of those lips on hers.

"Ah," he said, "but what if the rake reforms the lady instead?"

RUTH LANGAN

enjoys writing about modern men and women who are not afraid to be both strong and tender. Her sense of humor is evident in her work. Happily married to her childhood sweetheart, she thrives on the chaos created by two careers and five children.

RUTH LANGAN
Eden of Temptation

Silhouette Romance

Published by Silhouette Books New York

America's Publisher of Contemporary Romance

Silhouette Books by Ruth Langan

Just like Yesterday (ROM #121)
Hidden Isle (ROM #224)
Beloved Gambler (SE #119)
No Gentle Love (ROM #303)
Eden of Temptation (ROM #317)

 SILHOUETTE BOOKS, a Division of Simon & Schuster, Inc.
1230 Avenue of the Americas, New York, N.Y. 10020

Copyright © 1984 by Ruth Langan
Cover artwork copyright © 1984 Gary Maria

Distributed by Pocket Books

ISBN: 0-671-57317-9

First Silhouette Books printing September, 1984

10 9 8 7 6 5 4 3 2 1

Map by Ray Lundgren

To my children: Tom, Carol, Mary Margaret,
Pat, Mike
Chase your dreams

Eden of
Temptation

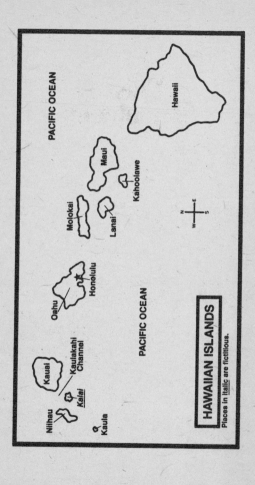

PACIFIC OCEAN

Hawaii

Maui

Kahoolawe

Molokai

Lanai

Oahu

Honolulu

PACIFIC OCEAN

Kauai

Keulakahi Channel

Kalai

Niihau

Kaula

HAWAIIAN ISLANDS

Places in italic are fictitious.

Chapter One

"Just below us is the Kaulakahi Channel, Dr. Lowry."

The Hawaiian pilot pointed to the window and his passenger forced herself to peer out cautiously. Far below churned the whitecaps of the Pacific.

He glanced at the young woman beside him. This small-boned creature, with fair hair pulled back in a severe knot at her nape and huge hazel eyes in a heart-shaped face, looked more like a wide-eyed teen than a famous botanist.

"Have you ever flown in a small plane before, doctor?"

She nodded her head. "Yes." For a few minutes, she had been absolutely terrified of the small craft. But Ann Lowry dealt with her fears the same way she had dealt with everything life handed her—by keeping a tight control over herself. When the little plane had lifted off the runway, she'd clutched her hands tightly together and forced herself to show absolutely no emotion. Control was the key. Control was everything. Control had kept her going when she'd found herself alone in the world. Control had kept her uncle from knowing how she really felt when he shut her out of his life. Control had kept her teaching at the university even though she sensed that most of her students would never share her love for nature. And through careful control, she could always manage to turn things around until, instead of fear, she felt acceptance and then optimism.

Her voice never wavered. "It's wonderful. I feel like a bird."

That's not a lie, she thought. *It's true. I'm free. Absolutely free.*

Cut loose from the academic life, the only life she had ever known. A continent away from her severest critic, her uncle. For a little while—for a whole month, in fact—adrift in uncharted territory.

I am not afraid. This will be a wonderful learning experience. She gritted her teeth.

A sudden downdraft caught the little plane, dropping it like an elevator out of control. The pilot saw the sudden motion as she gripped her hands tightly in her lap. Catching his look, she smiled shyly. "Well, maybe just a little afraid. But it's still exhilarating."

He smiled his approval at her gutsy determination.

The plane nosed heavenward, climbing above the thick clouds that boiled around them. After several minutes, it flew down through a gap in the clouds and entered a glorious patch of blue.

"There's your destination, Dr. Lowry. Kalai. The entire island is owned by the McFarland family. And there's the rain forest. Just below that tallest mountain peak."

The plane dropped very low, allowing her a closer glimpse of cool, misty forests and deep canyon walls. Between patches of red volcanic earth, she saw layers of ocher, rust and brown. Waterfalls created rivulets of molten silver in the afternoon sunlight.

Her heart quickened. All her years of study, all the papers she had written had been in preparation for this once-in-a-lifetime chance. She would have the opportunity to study, catalog and photograph plants that had rarely been seen by man.

Interspersed among the miles of lush vegetation, she spotted flocks of sheep and cattle and occasional huts.

"Does Dr. McFarland live in a native hut?"

The pilot chuckled. "The doctor and his family live in a big house. The only reason you see so many native huts is that he encourages everyone on the island to preserve the ancient Hawaiian way of life. This island is *kapu*, taboo, to all but those invited."

"Yes, I read that. In fact, I've read all I could find about the McFarlands. Fascinating people. Their Scottish ancestors were given this island by a Hawaiian king to be developed into a vast cattle empire, and the family has seen this lovely country go from the Stone Age to a monarchy to statehood in less than two hundred years. In the process, they've watched an entire way of life nearly disappear."

"There have been so many cultures here in my land."

The pilot smiled, widening the creases in his round face. "Japanese, Chinese, Polynesian, American, Filipino, Korean."

"And which are you?"

The smile became a laugh. "All of them, Dr. Lowry. All of them."

His look sobered as the wind whipped the plane's wings, tilting it a fraction. With both hands gripping the wheel, he steadied the craft.

Her own smile faded. "Moi, I'm so sorry I've made you late. I know I could have settled for the one piece of luggage and allowed the airline to deliver the other one when it was found. But it's simply not my nature to leave loose ends. I left home with two pieces of luggage, and I fully intended to arrive with two." Her own determined expression matched his. "Now, you'll be rushing the rest of the day to make up the lost time."

The pilot shrugged off her apology, intent now on the small island below. The little plane circled only once, then seemed to follow a course straight from the sun toward the narrow landing strip. At the last minute, the nose lifted slightly, and the wheels touched down with a faint puff of smoke at impact.

The man standing beside the jeep watched as the plane rolled to within a few feet of his vehicle.

The round face of the pilot broke into a wide smile, turning his eyes into narrow slits surrounded by creases. He gave the man on the runway a thumbs-up sign before turning to assist his passenger.

The door was flung open, the steps lowered. The man leaned against the hood of his car, watching with mild interest as his father's newest guest-scientist disem-barked.

Dressed in a drab, tailored suit, with her pristine blouse buttoned clear up to her throat, she clattered down the steps in sensible shoes. Over her shoulder hung a bag that looked as though it weighed more than she. With her hair drawn back in that simple knot, he couldn't be certain what color it was. Light brown. Faded blond. Very severe, he decided. Her eyes were hidden behind sunglasses.

Despite the shapeless clothes and the weight of the luggage, she moved with the artless grace of a child in a hurry. Impatient, he decided. Like so many of the scientific types he had come to know, she was restless to get on with it. And like those forced to spend long hours poring over scientific data, she had acquired that ability to govern her movements, to marshal all of her energies into a single task.

At the bottom of the steps she dropped her heavy burden and stared at him questioningly, forcing him into action. She had the feeling that he would have preferred to just stand there watching her, though she couldn't imagine why.

He stepped away from the car, extending his hand. "Dr. Lowry?"

She nodded and removed the glasses. Her eyes were striking, amber-colored and very big against her pale skin.

"I prefer Ann." She extended her hand. "And you are . . . ?"

Her voice seemed too young and breathless to belong

to the botanist whose biography had preceded her. He had given it only a cursory examination. Dry and academic, it told him little of the person—only her credentials, which were impressive.

"Jay McFarland." His big, tanned hand seemed to swallow hers in a strong handshake.

Feeling a shocking tingle course along her arm at their brief touch, she withdrew her palm and dropped it to her side. Meeting his direct gaze, she had an impression of a mountain of a man, his hair a bit too long, his cheeks and chin covered by a wild growth of red-brown beard. He looked like a fierce throwback to his ancestors in the Scottish Highlands, except in place of a kilt he wore frayed cut-offs and a flowery, native shirt.

"Ah. The son of Dr. Ian McFarland. I understand, doctor, that you're a practitioner of veterinary medicine."

She had done her homework well.

He smiled lazily. "Around here, I'm just Jamie McFarland, the island vet."

As the pilot handed down a suitcase, she said quickly, "I apologize for being so late. I hope you haven't had to wait here too long. I'm afraid the airline almost lost a valuable piece of luggage. It contained the clothing that had been recommended for use in my field trip to the rain forest. But more important, it contained all my notes."

"What's in there?" Jay pointed to the bag at her feet.

"My camera equipment, for slides of the plants I'll be studying. Thank goodness I didn't trust this to the luggage compartment of the plane. I couldn't possibly carry on my research without my equipment.''

"And that?" Jay indicated a garment bag as he lifted the suitcase and easily hefted the heavy camera bag in his other hand.

He heard the smile in her voice. "The winter boots and coat I was wearing when I left home."

"Boston, wasn't it?"

She nodded.

Jay turned to the pilot, who stood on the steps, waiting patiently.

"Want to ride back with us for some dinner before you fly out, Moi? It's been a long trip."

The pilot shook his head. "Not this time, Jamie. Got another passenger around nine tonight. Maybe next time."

The young woman offered her hand. "Thank you, Moi. I'm awfully sorry about holding you up like that. I was sure they'd find my bag. And I was right. I hope I haven't ruined your schedule."

"Don't worry," he said good-naturedly. "Here in the islands we're very relaxed. Schedules are things we write down, just so we have something to do. Afterwards we ignore them. But you'll soon find that out for yourself, Dr. Lowry. Good luck."

By the time the jeep was speeding along a trail cut through the lush vegetation the little plane was a mere speck in the sky.

With a spotless linen handkerchief Ann wiped the sheen from her forehead, wishing she could remove her suit jacket. The heat was stifling. But she wanted to appear professional when she met Dr. McFarland. After all, first impressions were so critical, and she truly wanted him to approve of her.

She turned to study the man at the wheel. He was a giant, with thick auburn hair that gleamed red in the brilliant sunshine, and skin bronzed from a lifetime beneath the Hawaiian sun. She felt intimidated by his size. Beside her he seemed a powerful animal.

"Do you live with your father, or do you and your wife have your own place?"

"I'm not married."

She tried to figure his age. Thirty. Thirty-five. Maybe younger. It was impossible to tell what his face would look like without that red beard.

"It was very kind of your father to invite me here."

He turned, and she thought he had the bluest eyes she had ever seen.

"He invites one scientist a year to explore our rain forest. You came highly recommended by your peers."

"Then I hope I live up to their recommendations. I know how much your father values his privacy. I'd hate to be the one to cause him to discontinue this program. It means so much to science to be able to study species that have become extinct in the rest of the world. Your rain forest is a treasurehouse of knowledge to the scientific community."

He turned his head, pinning her with those laughing blue eyes. "Do you always talk like that?"

"Like what?"

"Like a textbook. You sound like you're lecturing in a classroom."

She flushed and stared down at her hands. She had often thought that her students secretly laughed at her behind her back. But in her presence, no one had ever before made fun of her manner of speaking. She knew she appeared rather prim and formal to strangers. But that was the way her uncle had raised her. In his household there had never been a slang expression allowed. In her classroom at the university, though she was actually younger than some of her graduate students, she seemed much older. It wasn't an artificial formality. She simply knew no other way.

"I'll try not to lecture too often, Dr. McFarland."

"My father is Dr. McFarland. I prefer Jay."

"All right . . . Jay."

Embarrassed, she decided to forego any further attempt at conversation. Feeling extremely uncomfortable with this man, she turned to stare at the tropical paradise surrounding them. But he was impossible to ignore.

He seemed so relaxed, as if he had nothing more important to do than drive this jeep. He seemed too . . . earthy. She was accustomed to bookish men who could discuss art and politics and especially science. She frowned. With that roguish gleam in his eye, he would probably prefer to discuss the mating habits of the island goats.

Her gaze wandered over the lush undergrowth. It seemed incredible that a mere twelve hours ago she had been slogging through several feet of snow. Now her summer-weight suit was far too heavy for this climate.

In the last few hours, she had thrilled to the sight of

Diamond Head rising over Honolulu and felt a lump lodge in her throat as the plane had passed over Pearl Harbor toward the Honolulu Airport. After switching to the small interisland plane, she had passed over a satellite tracking station on a remote island, reminding her that civilization was swiftly encroaching on this once primitive archipelago which stretched for nearly sixteen hundred miles in the Pacific.

The road they were following was barely more than a path cut through the jungle. In places the sun was completely hidden beneath a canopy of vines and foliage that twisted and merged into a tapestry of greens and yellows and brilliant hues of red and orange.

Without realizing it the scientist in her took over. Ann grew intent on mentally listing every variety of plant she could identify. To her trained eye this lush tropical paradise was a garden of delights.

"Frangipani. Bird of Paradise. Oh, Glory Bush." Her head swiveled as the jeep moved past a clump of brilliant star-shaped flowers. "Passion Vine. Lovely."

The driver slowed, watching the intense look on her face slowly dissolve into a smile.

"Heaven." She expelled a long sigh. "I've died and gone to heaven," she whispered, staring at the Cassia's feathery green foliage and bright yellow blossoms sweep past their vehicle.

As she turned her head, a patch of sunlight caught her in its beam like a floodlight.

Softest blond, he thought, studying her gleaming tawny hair. The color of newborn fawns that roam the forest. Her skin looked as though it had never seen the sun. Its pale ivory color gave her a delicate, almost fragile appearance. Small, intense and private, he decided. Her openness to nature's beauty was in direct contrast to the face she presented to the world. She would give away very little of herself, he thought. She kept the private person hidden behind a wall of reserve. Interesting. And very bright. Suddenly, the month that loomed ahead of them seemed more a challenge than he had anticipated.

Without warning, they emerged from the jungle trail into brilliant sunlight. Spread before them were rolling hills of green, dotted with palm trees and planted with a dazzling array of native flowers and plants. At the top of a hill stood a sprawling, two-story house, with an orange tile roof and open, latticed verandas on each level encircling the front and sides.

As they drove nearer Ann could see wicker furniture, upholstered in cool green floral cotton patterns, set about the front porch.

"Oh, doctor . . . Jay, your home is beautiful."

He smiled, and she noticed the tiny laugh lines about his eyes.

"Yes, it is. I suppose sometimes I take it for granted. Having been born here I forget how it must look to a *malihini*."

Seeing her eyebrows arch in a question, he added, "That means stranger."

"*Malihini*." She tried out the new word, liking the way it rolled off her tongue. "I hope I won't be a *malihini* for long."

His eyes swept over her, causing the heat to rush to

her cheeks. "I'm sure you won't. We pride ourselves on being the warmest hosts in the world."

She was grateful that he jumped from the parked jeep at that moment and bent to her luggage. She wasn't accustomed to having men stare at her. It was a strange, awkward feeling that caused her cheeks to flame and her heart to race. For most of her life, Ann Lowry had been thought of as the brain of the class, or a bit of an eccentric, a girl who loved her plants more than people. That only reinforced the lesson her uncle had taught her years earlier—that his ward should concentrate on her studies if she wanted to be pleasing to him.

A stunning little girl of about twelve, with waist-length black hair and sparkling almond-shaped eyes, burst through the front door and rushed to Jay's side.

"Let me carry something, Doc Jamie."

"In a minute. First, Shrimp, come meet our house-guest."

He turned to his passenger. "Dr. Ann Lowry, this is Laela, the granddaughter of our housekeeper."

Ann extended her hand. "Hello, Laela. It's nice to meet you."

"I'm happy to meet you too, doctor." The child turned to Jay with eyes dancing in undisguised delight. "She's no bigger than me. How can she be a doctor?"

Jay tousled her hair. "Because she studied hard. Unlike someone I know."

"Oh, Doc Jamie. Don't start that again. Give me something to carry inside."

"Here Shrimp, try this."

He thrust the camera bag into her arms and watched

with amusement as she struggled under its weight. Her eyes grew round. "What's in here? An anchor?"

He laughed. "The doctor's camera gear. Give it back, Shrimp. I'll let you carry the garment bag."

Laela accepted the bag from his hands and ran ahead to hold the door.

As they crossed the open veranda and stepped into the coolness beyond Jay murmured, "Welcome to our bonnie home, Dr. Lowry."

It was such an unexpected contrast to hear the Scottish word used on this Hawaiian island that Ann found her mouth drop open in surprise before she could compose herself. "Thank you."

She glanced around, noting the ceiling fan slowly turning, cooling the bright airy room whose tile floors gleamed with fresh polish. The furniture was a mix of leather and old wood, highlighted with a few chairs covered in bright plaid. A grandfather clock chimed the hour as they entered, and Ann studied the intricate carving, instantly liking the ageless feeling of the clock and this house.

Jay left the bags at the foot of the stairs and beckoned Ann toward a set of double doors off the foyer. "My father is in the study," he said, opening the doors and standing aside for her.

As she brushed past him he seemed to lean down, inhaling her soft feminine smell.

A lion's mane of white hair was bent over an open book resting on a polished desktop. The head lifted, and pale blue eyes examined the young woman walking toward him.

"Dad, this is Dr. Ann Lowry. Ann, my father, Dr. Ian McFarland."

She stepped closer, extending her hand. The older man slowly pushed himself from the chair, standing stiffly before formally accepting the handshake.

The straight aquiline nose, the blue eyes and the wide forehead were the same as those of the giant son. His eyes crinkled as he smiled, and she found herself wondering if Jay's mouth and chin would be the same beneath his beard.

"Well, well. Dr. Lowry. It's happy we are that you've come to do your research. Most impressive record." He glanced at his son, then returned his searching look to her. "I must confess, I expected someone a bit older. You've managed to accomplish much in your young years."

She smiled and said nothing. How many times had she heard these same words? It seemed that everyone expected a dedicated scientist to be old.

She flashed him an impish grin as a thought struck. "From what I've read of you, Dr. McFarland, you were the youngest ornithologist to ever conduct research on the giant condor. If it weren't for your early work, that bird would now be extinct."

He nodded, smiling. *"Touché.* Thank goodness for young scientists, Dr. Lowry. They're never willing to accept statistics at face value." He pointed to a chair. "Please, sit and be comfortable."

Ann sat down, aware that Jay stood near the bay window, observing without joining in the conversation.

She had the distinct impression that he was studying her carefully, but she forced herself not to glance over at him. Trying to avoid his eyes she bent down, placing her attaché case on the floor at her feet.

"Do you have any specific goals while you're doing your work in the field, Dr. Lowry?"

She gave a wry smile. "Probably too many to accomplish all of them. I've heard that there are over twenty thousand different varieties of orchid alone in your rain forest. If I can identify even one or two that have never before been seen, I'll be happy. But I suppose every scientist wants to be the first to discover something." She moistened her lips with the tip of her tongue. "Doctor, I'm trying not to get too excited about this. But the truth is, I can't wait to spend a whole month doing field research with a man of your incredible reputation. You have studied this rain forest for most of your life. You've worked with and taught the best in the world. Just being able to listen to you, to absorb some of your information, will be enough reward."

The older man cleared his throat. Standing slowly, he reached behind his chair and grasped a cane. Instantly his son was at his side, offering his strong arm. The first thing Ann was aware of was the fact that both men stood like giants, well over six feet. Two pairs of smiling blue eyes were regarding her with barely concealed amusement. It was a moment longer before she realized what this was leading to.

"As you can see, Dr. Lowry, I am no longer capable of doing field research."

She caught her breath, embarrassed by her mistake.

"It's been a number of years since I went into the rain forest."

"I'm sorry, Dr. McFarland. I just . . ."

"Nonsense. Think nothing of it. It happens all the time. I still enjoy being around my fellow scientists and talking endlessly about our favorite subjects. But I can no longer do the work of a young researcher." He smiled at his son, standing proudly beside him. "Jamie here will be your guide through our rain forest. He obliges me by taking a month off his own work each year just so I can continue this program."

Ann licked her lips and forced a smile. "I see. Well, that's very kind of you . . . Jay." Her hands twisted together awkwardly.

The red beard twitched in amusement, watching her determined control. Except for the hands and the wide amber eyes that seemed to have grown even larger, she was hiding her discomfort well.

"Jamie's a wonderful guide. He knows every inch of that jungle out there. He's been going out into the field with me since he was just a lad. You'll be in good hands."

"I'm sure I will be."

The older man seemed satisfied. "Now. I expect you'd like to freshen up before dinner. As I recall, that's an exhausting trip from Boston." He smiled at someone beyond her, and Ann turned to see a plump woman in a huge flowing muumuu.

"Mala. This is Dr. Lowry, our visiting botanist. Will you show her to her room?"

The old woman smiled, showing a row of white, even teeth. With hands on her hips she regarded their guest. "So little. No bigger than Laela. How can this little girl be a scientist?"

The two men laughed.

Ian McFarland leaned heavily on his son's arm. "You'll get used to Mala, Dr. Lowry. She mothers everyone. Including me."

Ann followed the woman to the stairs and had begun ascending behind her to the second-floor rooms when she realized she had left her attaché case behind.

"Oh. Mala. Just a moment. I'll be right back."

Hurrying to the study, she paused at the open door as she heard her name mentioned. Embarrassed, she stopped, wondering whether she should rush in and pretend she hadn't heard the voice, or knock in order to let them know she was about to overhear their conversation.

". . . think of our guest? Do you anticipate any problems?"

Ann raised her fist to the open door. The deeper timbre of Jay's voice kept her from knocking.

"She looks like she'd blow away in a good wind. I'm not at all certain she can withstand the rigors of the rain forest."

"Nonsense. Dr. Smythe-Fielding gave her his highest recommendations. I realize she's a bit young, but she seems a bright, pretty little thing, eh?"

A smile of satisfaction curved her lips, then disappeared instantly at Jay's response.

"I hadn't noticed." He bit off the words.

"You, Jamie! Losing your touch, man?"

She heard the teasing laughter in the old man's voice.

"So prim and proper, Dad. In terms that only an old birdwatcher like yourself could understand, a bit of a sparrow, I think. Too drab for my taste."

"Ah, but you know what they say . . ."

She stifled a gasp and turned away, humiliated at overhearing their private conversation.

Subdued, she climbed the stairs and allowed old Mala to show her around her suite of rooms. Proudly, the woman showed her the open veranda, furnished with a white wicker chair and lounge upholstered in a lovely pink floral cotton. In the bedroom the large bed was covered in a matching pink floral quilt. In one corner stood a Victorian dressing mirror and two pink-striped side chairs. The bathroom of white marble boasted pink towels and a fluffy rug. The footed tub was flanked by tall ferns in white marble planters. It was the sort of luxury Ann had dreamed of all her life. But it was entirely foreign to her austere background. This was the sort of room girls dreamed in, but never worked or actually lived in. And for tonight, it was hers. She should have been overwhelmed. But as the old woman unpacked, then left her guest alone to bathe and rest before dinner, Ann gave in to the sting of Jay's words.

Settling into a lukewarm tub, she fumed. A drab sparrow. That really was an apt description. Hadn't her uncle always felt much the same way? The only time he had ever noticed her was when she brought home her report card. It was the one area where she could shine for him. And from her earliest years with him she had learned that his approval could only be won by beating all her classmates academically.

As she lathered the fragrant pink soap, she steeled herself. She had better beware. This setting, this paradise was only make-believe. Reality for her was research, scientific studies and papers, and a return to the academic life.

Stepping from the tub, she let down her tawny, shoulder-length hair, brushed it vigorously and cinched a simple terry robe before climbing beneath the sheets.

One month. One long month with a man who found her dull and drab. It should prove to be nothing new to her. Hadn't her path always been like this? He was just one more obstacle. She had been in paradise for barely an hour and already had found a serpent. Found herself stuck with a mountain of a man who would probably make her job as difficult as possible. As always, she would have to find a way to deal with it. And deal with it she would. Hard work and discipline were a comfort to her. Control. Cool control. It always worked.

Exhausted, she slept.

Chapter Two

"Laela."

The young girl paused in the act of placing a pile of neatly folded linens on a shelf in the hallway and smiled at their houseguest.

"Yes, Dr. Lowry."

"Would you come in here a moment?"

The girl glanced around the airy bedroom, abloom with pink touches. "Did I wake you? Doc Jamie said I must be very quiet so you could rest."

Ann smiled at the girl's earnest expression. "No, Laela, you didn't wake me. I enjoyed a good nap, but I've been awake for a little while now. I need your opinion about something."

The girl was impressed. An important houseguest needed her. "What can I do, Dr. Lowry?"

"The first thing you can do is stop calling me Dr. Lowry. It makes me sound like someone old and important. Please call me Ann."

"Oh, I'm not sure Grandmother would allow it."

"Don't worry." Ann paused. "I'll explain to your grandmother."

Laela stood beside the slender woman, mentally measuring herself against Ann, enjoying the fact that they were nearly the same size. "Well, I suppose I could call you Ann. If my grandmother doesn't mind."

"That's fine." Ann sat on the edge of her bed and patted it. As the girl joined her, Ann asked, "Laela, do they dress for dinner here?"

Laela was so serious, Ann had to stifle a laugh. "Oh yes . . . Ann. You must wear clothes. No one here has ever gone to dinner undressed."

Covering her mouth with her hand Ann jumped up and crossed the room, hoping Laela wouldn't see her laughter. When she turned back she had the laughter under control.

"Thank you, Laela. Will I see you at dinner?"

"Yes. I already ate, but I'll help my grandmother in the kitchen before I start my homework."

"Is there a fully staffed school here on the island?"

"Yes. And high school too. But for the university we have to leave the island and go to the big island. Or the mainland."

"Do many leave for the university?"

The girl's head bobbed, and she unself-consciously flicked her long hair behind her. "Yes. It's hard to leave here. But we understand that it's the only way we can learn to be what we want." She grinned proudly. "I'm going to be a vet like Doc Jamie."

Ann saw the shining look of love in the little girl's eyes and wondered how a big, gruff bear-of-a-man like Jay could inspire such loyalty.

"Do you ever watch him work with the animals?"

"Sometimes, when I don't have to be in school, he lets me go with him. I already know a lot about animals." She paused as a new thought intruded. "Doc Jamie says a botanist is a plant doctor. Is that a lot like an animal doctor?"

Ann laughed, liking the fresh way this girl's mind worked. "Yes, I guess I am a plant doctor. Except that I can't make them well if they get sick. All I can do is study them, catalog them and learn, from scientific studies, how they can be of service to man."

"I don't understand."

Ann smiled gently. "I guess it does seem a strange way to spend one's life. But I believe that plants hold the secrets to life. In time, scientists like myself believe we can alter plant genes, to produce plants so sturdy they can thrive under the most adverse conditions. And that in turn would lead to erasing world hunger. Too many innocent people today are subjected to a very cruel death."

She was aware that the girl beside her had suddenly stiffened at the word death. Her voice took on a softer tone. "I notice that you live with your grandmother. Are your parents here on the island, Laela?"

Her dark head shook slightly. "They're both dead."

Huge dark eyes met Ann's questioning gaze. "They drowned in a storm."

Ann's arm instinctively went around the young shoulders. "How long ago?"

"Last summer."

Ann's voice was little more than a murmur. "How old are you, Laela?"

"Twelve."

For long moments, Ann stroked the silken hair, her voice muffled against the top of the girl's head. It was a rare thing for her to put aside her reserve and display this tender side of her nature. But Laela touched her deeply. "It will hurt for a very long time. But like a deep, painful cut, it will heal over. Of course, there's always scar tissue. And sometimes at the most unexpected moments you'll feel a stab of pain, and the hurt will be fresh again. You're very lucky, Laela, to have so many people around you who love you."

The girl swallowed. "How can you know what I'm feeling? Nobody else understands how I feel."

Ann paused for a deep breath. "I also lost my parents in an accident when I was only twelve."

Laela shot her an incredulous look. "You did?" She studied the woman beside her, as if seeing her in a new light. "Did you have a grandmother to love you?"

Ann shook her head softly. "No. An uncle."

"Was he as funny as Doc Jamie?"

Ann smiled, noting again the almost reverential tone at the mention of his name. "I'm afraid my uncle bore no resemblance to Jay McFarland."

"I love Doc Jamie," Laela breathed.

Ann looked into the shining face and knew the child meant those words. She stood. "Well now, young lady, I think I'd better get dressed and downstairs for dinner."

"I'll see you in a little while." Like a whirlwind the girl picked up the pile of linens and hurried to the door. In the doorway she paused and blurted, "I like your hair down like that, Ann. It looks all soft and golden."

Before Ann could react, the girl was gone.

Crossing to the closet, Ann studied her prim navy cotton sundress with matching crisp white jacket. When she had bought it in Boston it had looked almost festive. Now, here on this colorful island, it looked as drab and colorless as the rest of her wardrobe.

The only other clothes in the closet were several pairs of khaki pants and shirts, which Ann had brought to wear in the rain forest.

Hurriedly, she pulled on the sundress. The back was cut very low and the narrow spaghetti straps made wearing a bra impossible, but she would be covered by the matching jacket.

The only dress shoes she had brought were the sensible pumps she had worn on the plane. Along with them she had high army boots for the trek through the jungle and two pairs of sneakers. That left no choice. The leather pumps seemed a little incongruous with the sundress but, she thought as she began pulling her hair into a neat knot, who would notice?

Jay. The thought prickled. He had already decided she was a sparrow. This would only confirm it.

So what! She dropped the brush with a clatter and studied the hair swirling about her face. For one brief moment, recalling Laela's compliment, she considered leaving it down. Then habit took over. She always wore her hair in a knot. It was professional. Just because she was on a tropical island now, her circumstances hadn't changed. She was here to do a job, not join a charm school.

With more energy than it called for, she wound her hair into a severe bun, then hung her terry robe in the closet. She didn't care what Jay McFarland thought of her. He was nothing more than her guide during the field trip. They didn't have to make scintillating conversation. They didn't even have to like each other. All she needed from him was competence. All he needed from her was the ability to keep from getting lost in the jungle. He had told his father she looked like she'd blow away in a good wind. She would show Jay McFarland a thing or two about inner strength.

She applied some lip gloss and studied her face critically. Too pale. She touched some color to her cheeks and shook her head in defeat. Her eyes were too big, her nose too small. Her light eyebrows and gold-tipped lashes were almost lost against the luminous skin. Her uncle used to call her the little mouse. It was true. She was thin to the point of being nearly shapeless. She had no sense of style. Hopeless. With a last glance, she turned from the mocking mirror and made her way down the stairs.

Ian McFarland and his son were enjoying the last of the late afternoon sun on an open, brick-paved court-yard. Fragrant hibiscus draped over a low brick wall, lending perfume to the spectacular scene. Crimson ribbons trailed the waves of the Pacific as the orange globe of the sun hovered just above the horizon.

"Ah, Dr. Lowry. Come join us and relax before dinner. What will you drink?" Despite his infirmity Ian McFarland heaved himself heavily to his feet upon her arrival.

Ann felt a rush of emotion at his courtly manners.

"Whatever you're having, doctor."

"Can you handle scotch and soda?"

She nodded. She had learned to adapt to a man's world at a very early age. "That will be fine."

Jay fixed the drink and handed it to her. Still smarting from the words she had overheard earlier, she accepted it with a brief thank you.

He continued to stand beside her, making her uncomfortably aware of his great size. To escape him she sat down in a wicker chair and faced his father.

"Your home is lovely, doctor. And from what I saw of your island from the air, I know I'm going to like it."

"That's a rough flight. Do you fly well, doctor?"

She lowered her eyes a moment, avoiding the question. "Please call me Ann, Dr. McFarland."

"All right, Ann." He waited, then asked, "Was it a rough flight?"

"No. It wasn't too bad."

Jay watched her hands tighten around the glass.

"How do you like your rooms?"

"They're lovely. I've never been in anything quite so elegant. It's a good thing I'm going into the field—I think I could get spoiled if I spent much time here. I don't know how you manage to get any work done in this paradise, doctor.''

He smiled indulgently. ''I suppose we're like children living in an ice cream factory. After a while, we begin to take all this for granted. Then we discipline ourselves to turn out the work required.'' He lifted his glass in his son's direction. ''Look at the brilliant papers Jamie manages to write, despite his hectic schedule.''

Stunned, Ann turned her head to study Jay, who was leaning a hip against the brick wall, one leg crossed carelessly over the other. He met her look with a lopsided grin.

''I'm sorry. I'm not familiar with your work.'' She turned back to his father. ''Jay told me he's just the local vet.''

Ian McFarland chuckled. ''I certainly can't attribute that to his extreme modesty, because Jamie's always been flamboyant. So it must be that he was having fun with you, Ann. I'm afraid he's a terrible tease.'' He looked down a moment, then added with a gleam in his eye, ''It runs in the family.''

A billowing muumuu, the size of a small tent, appeared in the doorway. Smilingly, Mala announced dinner.

Ian McFarland supported himself on his cane and gallantly offered his arm to Ann. Together they walked to the dining room, leaving Jay to follow.

Like all the rooms she had seen so far, the dining room was large and airy, with a floor of dark, polished tile and a gleaming, glass-topped table, around which were scattered white wicker chairs with gaily colored floral cushions. A bowl of fragrant hibiscus and multicolored wild orchids graced the center of the table.

Laela entered, carrying a tray of salad bowls. Like her grandmother she was dressed in a flowing gown of swirling pinks and mauves, woven into the most beautiful fabric Ann had ever seen. Instead of being styled like a traditional muumuu, it had long tapered sleeves and a mandarin collar edged with black braid. Black frog closings paraded diagonally down the bodice. Her gleaming black hair and dark eyes were a perfect contrast to the soft colors.

"Oh, Laela. You look beautiful."

The little girl gave Ann a warm smile.

"Thank you. Doc Jamie bought this for my birthday."

Surprise showed on Ann's face. Jay McFarland didn't look like the kind of man who would know or care about female attire.

She glanced at him from beneath a fringe of lashes, and realized he was staring at her. Embarrassed, she looked away quickly.

As Ann lifted her fork to her mouth, Laela said without warning, "People from Boston don't wear any clothes."

The fork clattered against her plate.

"What?" Jay studied the child with a bemused expression. "What are you saying, Laela?"

"Ann—Dr. Lowry asked me if she had to dress for dinner. It's a good thing she asked. Otherwise she'd be awfully embarrassed when she came downstairs." Laela finished refilling a water glass, then held her serving tray at her side. In a serious tone, she added, "I told her everyone here has to wear clothes."

Ann and her hosts sat in complete silence.

When the young girl walked from the room with a jaunty air of importance, three heads swiveled to the closed door. After another moment of protracted silence, there was an explosion of raucous laughter.

Ann watched in humiliation as the two men wiped tears of laughter from their eyes. A stain as crimson as the hibiscus on the table colored her throat and cheeks.

When she finally found her voice, she muttered, "I knew she misunderstood my question, but I didn't have the heart to correct her. Now I wish I had."

"And deny us our heartiest laugh of the day?" Ian lifted a glass of pale wine. "My dear Ann, I'm so glad you are tender-hearted. Even though the joke was at your expense."

Avoiding Jay's laughing eyes, she smiled at Ian and tasted the wine. Light and fruity, it was a delicate compliment to the roasted fowl and fresh vegetables. As hungry as she was, Ann found it difficult to eat with Jay seated across from her. Each time she looked up his gaze rested on her cheeks, which still bore a slight flush. Throughout the meal his lips wore a smile, as if he were still enjoying Laela's remarks.

Ann refused the sherbert and nibbled fresh pineapple for dessert. Settling back with strong hot coffee, she sighed.

"Do you realize that if I were still in Boston, I'd probably be shoveling snow out my driveway right now?"

"Do you live alone?" Ian asked.

"Yes. I own a small house near the campus where I teach."

"Wouldn't you feel safer in an apartment building, with other residents?"

She could feel Jay's intense look and she resisted the urge to meet his gaze. Instead, she feigned interest in the pattern on the place mat.

"I wanted something of my own."

"But how do you manage to maintain a house while you work?"

She glanced at Ian's skeptical expression. "When I'm not teaching or doing my research, I spend most of my time keeping up the house. There are a lot of hours to fill in a big city, Dr. McFarland."

"So there are." He stood and reached for his cane. "Let's take our brandy in the study. I think you'll enjoy seeing some of my latest papers, Ann."

She followed him, aware of Jay's presence directly behind her. When they reached the study, Jay held the door and inhaled the delicate fragrance of her perfume as she passed.

While Jay fixed their drinks, she settled into a comfortable leather chair and pulled on wire-rimmed reading glasses. The older man seemed eager for her reaction as she read the paper he had labored over for the past months.

Jay's gaze drifted from Ann's white throat, visible beneath the jacket of her dress, upward to her fair hair gleaming in the glow of the reading lamp.

She read quickly, intensely, turning each page without a pause until she had finished.

"This is wonderful, doctor. I'm sure the scientific community thought this bird was near total extinction. If there are enough for breeding purposes, some could actually be relocated in other tropical countries. You must be ecstatic about this discovery."

The older man beamed. "Yes, I am. Of course, the discovery isn't mine alone. I had help from Dr. Coulter of UCLA, who spent several months tracking this bird. He then brought in a team of students to help him. The entire project took two years."

"And it was all possible because you made your rain forest available for their scientific explorations. You must be very proud, doctor."

"Humble, Ann. It's wonderful to be able to offer such a treasure to my associates."

While the older man spoke of the accomplishments of some of the earlier teams of scientists and naturalists who had been invited to the island, Ann slipped off her shoes and tucked her feet beneath her. Sipping brandy, listening to a man who had spent his entire life in a quest for knowledge, Ann felt she had truly found paradise. She experienced a stab of regret when the older man finally pulled himself to his feet.

"I'm afraid I must excuse myself now. Ann, it's been delightful talking with you. I enjoy bright, searching minds like yours. Tomorrow we'll talk some more. Jamie and I both feel that you need one more day to acclimate yourself before taking on the rigors of the rain forest. And Jamie himself has just come back from an extensive tour of the island, tying up a lot of loose ends before taking the next month off." The old man shot his son a look of love. "That's why he looks like such a barbarian. There's no way a man can get a shave or haircut while he's busy taking care of thousands of sheep and cattle." He bowed slightly at the doorway. "Goodnight, my dear. It's been a very pleasant evening. Goodnight, son."

Ann felt trapped by the sudden silence of the room. It was stifling. With Ian there had been so much to talk about. With his son she felt awkward and tongue-tied.

"Would you like to walk through the gardens?"

She nodded, relieved. Wriggling her feet into the pumps, she stood eagerly. Under the cover of darkness he wouldn't be able to see her discomfort.

He held the door to the patio and again Ann brushed past him, unaware of his reaction to the delicate scent of her perfume.

"Oh, this is lovely." Ann stared at the midnight sky, adorned by the jewels of a million stars.

"Wait until you experience the morning mist of the rain forest. It's incredible."

She turned her face to him. His voice had grown softer, to match the velvet night.

"You made my father feel young tonight."

"I did?"

"Umm." He held a lighter to his cigar, and the flame illuminated his bold features for a moment before he snapped it shut. "The way you hung on his every word.

He needs that sometimes. He misses the camaraderie of his fellow scientists."

"He has you."

"I'm away a lot. We have vast cattle and sheep ranches on the island. And though my assistant Kai is a great help, I'm the only vet."

"You seem . . ." She was instantly sorry that she had started. Now she was obliged to finish her sentence. She searched her mind for a polite phrase. ". . . so easygoing. As if you haven't a care in the world. I guess my first impression was that you did very little here."

He chuckled low in his throat. The sound sent tremors along her spine. "What you're really saying, little Annie Laurie, is that you thought I was a lazy bum, sponging off my famous father's money."

She was grateful for the darkness that hid her flaming cheeks. "I didn't say that."

"You didn't have to. Your eyes are very expressive, did you know?"

She turned away, horrified. As she moved across the patio she could feel him close behind her.

At the sound of a low-flying plane, they both looked up.

"Is someone coming here?"

He shook his head. "We don't get many uninvited guests. Probably going to one of the nearby islands. You'll see plenty of small planes flying overhead. That's the principal form of travel in this remote area."

When she looked down he had moved so close they were touching. She was aware of his flowery Hawaiian

shirt brushing her arm, and the scent of his tobacco
mixed with the wonderful floral scents of the exotic
blooms in the garden.

His hand reached out and caught a tiny wisp of her
hair which had come loose in the soft breeze. Wrapping
it around his finger, he turned her head to a shaft of silver
moonlight and studied her eyes, which seemed too big
for her face.

Her heartbeat accelerated. She wanted to bolt, but that
would be too cowardly. She tried her best defense—cool
control. Meeting his gaze, she asked, "Why did you call
me Annie Laurie?"

"You don't know the song?"

She shook her head.

"I'll sing it for you sometime. It's about a lovely
Scottish lass." His voice lowered to nearly a whisper.
"'. . . and for bonnie Annie Laurie, I'd lay me down
and die.'"

Like a willow, he was bending toward her. There was
no doubt about his intentions. His blue eyes sought the
amber flame of her eyes, drawing her to him like a
magnet.

She found herself anticipating the kiss. A little afraid,
but curious. She had kissed men. He certainly wouldn't
be the first. But Jay McFarland wasn't like other
men. She didn't know why. She only knew it was
true.

His fingertips caressed her cheek. Strong fingers.
They lifted her chin, and then his lips brushed hers,
tasting her, allowing her to taste him.

She breathed in the heady, male scent of him. There

was a hint of brandy on his lips, and the taste of tobacco. She had never dreamed anything could be so sweet.

She started to pull back, and suddenly his hands clutched her shoulders, drawing her firmly to him. The kiss was cataclysmic. Her universe was rocking violently, opening up and enveloping her in something new and unexplored.

His hands slipped beneath her jacket, burning a trail of fire on her bare back. She stiffened for a moment, shocked at the touch of his fingertips against her sensitive skin. Then he drew her close against him, and she melted into his arms. His kiss was easy, practiced, and although she felt awkward he made it seem right.

When he lifted his lips from hers she stood in his embrace, unable to move. Wide eyes stared into his. She saw his eyes narrow perceptibly, regarding her with a look she couldn't fathom.

As soft as a whisper, he brushed his lips over hers, as if to confirm what they had both felt. The red beard, which she had thought looked so rough, was soft against her skin. She had an overpowering desire to reach up and run her fingers through it. Instead, she clutched his waist, wanting the kiss to go on, wanting it to end and wondering what was happening to her common sense.

With his fingers beneath her chin, he lifted her face for his inspection. He studied her features as if memorizing them.

"Bonnie little Annie."

She flushed. "Doesn't bonnie mean beautiful?" Her voice seemed strained. She was surprised at how difficult it was to speak.

"Yes." He smiled.

"Then you have the wrong Annie."

She tried to pull away but he caught her firmly by the shoulders, holding her against him. When she tried to turn her face away he caught her chin, forcing her to look at him.

"I said bonnie. Aye, and I meant bonnie." His firm tone took on the Scottish burr of his ancestors.

"Let me go, Jay."

Reluctantly he dropped his hands to his sides.

Primly she adjusted her jacket, pulling it firmly about her.

She caught his mocking smile.

"Bonnie Annie, I believe you may have forgotten to put on one rather . . . intimate item of apparel this evening."

Her mouth opened in surprise.

"Not that I'm complaining, mind you. You felt very good in my arms. The less armor the better."

"I won't dignify that comment with a reply." She was grateful he couldn't see her cheeks burning in embarrassment.

As she turned to walk away, his next words stopped her. "Before you go up to your room, Ann, stop in the library and get your attaché case. Otherwise you may have to stand outside the door and eavesdrop again."

Her eyes widened. Regaining her composure, she stammered, "You mean you knew all along that I was out there?"

He nodded, a smile twitching beneath the red beard.

"You said those awful things about me on purpose?"

He chuckled. "My father did warn you that there's a bit of the tease in both of us."

"How did you know I was there?"

He walked closer and drew in his breath. "Because, little Annie, your perfume is very distinct. Delicate, floral, like the little Passion Flower you'll see in the rain forest." His voice dropped to a seductive purr. "I'd know you even in the dark."

His words caused a pulse to flutter deep inside her.

Chapter Three

For long hours, Ann lay awake in her bed, replaying the scene with Jay.

What was there about the man that so intrigued her? He was unlike anyone she had ever met. His sense of humor was outrageous. A real dedication to his work belied that air of lazy indifference—or so his father said. She had her doubts that a man who appeared that easygoing could actually be ambitious. And he was too earthy for her taste; he was almost blatantly sexual. It frightened her. And tantalized her. The thought of being held in his arms taunted her, until she found herself prowling the room, searching for something to occupy her mind.

For several hours she read from a scientific journal, until the words began to blur. Crawling into bed she found herself still lying awake, recalling the touch of Jay's lips on hers.

"So. You're finally awake. How did you sleep, little doctor?"

Ann sat propped up in bed, several plump pillows beneath her head. She had opened the drapes to allow the sunshine to bathe the room in its glow. From her bed she could see the verdant, rolling hills. It was the most luxurious feeling she had ever known, to recline among the bedclothes with nothing more important on the agenda than to watch the beauty of nature resplendent all around her.

She sighed. "I slept well, Mala. This is such a beautiful room."

"Jamie said we shouldn't disturb you. He said your body would still be on mainland time."

The rotund housekeeper seemed to drift across the room, her feet unseen beneath the voluminous skirt of her everpresent muumuu. She placed a stack of fresh pink towels in the bathroom.

"Would you like some fruit and coffee in your room while you dress, or would you rather wait until you come downstairs later?"

Ann's needs had never been catered to with such care. It was a wickedly sensuous pleasure.

"Thank you, Mala. I'll just wait until I'm dressed, and have some coffee downstairs."

"Whatever you say, little doctor." The housekeeper's hands rested on her enormous hips, eyeing the tiny figure in the bed. "But I think you should eat more. You're no bigger than a minnow."

The smile of pleasure stayed on Ann's face while she bathed and dressed. Such luxury. If she spent too much time here she'd be spoiled. It was a good thing she was leaving on the field trip in the morning. A month in the rain forest ought to keep her from feeling too pampered.

A month with Jay McFarland. As she wrapped her freshly washed hair in a towel she stared at her reflection in the mirror.

What did he see when he looked at her? She studied the wide, hazel eyes that changed color with her moods or clothes. Sometimes softest green when she was in a pensive mood, they could glow like a cat's amber eyes when she was angry or aroused. But Ann was unaware of their intensity. She only saw eyes that probably gave away too much emotion. She would have to beware. She pursed her mouth in a pout of concentration. Lips that were a little too full for her small face. It didn't matter that a man might find them full and sensuous, the sort of lips that begged a kiss. High cheekbones that would probably be described as hollow. Models might die for such cheeks, but Ann thought of them only as too bony. She made a face at herself, aware that she was groping for something that would logically explain his actions last night.

With a sigh she turned away from her image. He probably saw a plain scientist who was responsible for taking him away from his work for a whole month.

Running a comb through the tangles she tried to

concentrate on something, anything besides Jay. She was anxious about seeing him again. Eager, yet afraid. In the light of day would he look at the little mouse he had held in his arms last night and wonder what had possessed him to do such a thing?

It seemed forever before her hair was blown dry and fastened into a neat knot. This morning Ann seemed all thumbs. She applied her makeup carefully, deciding against adding color to cheeks that were already blushing at the thought of the man downstairs.

There was nothing to wear except the skirt to her dark suit, and a simple summery blouse. She wished now she had thought to buy some frivolous clothes before the trip. But the truth was she wouldn't know how to buy that sort of thing. Her closet back in Boston was filled with somber, practical clothes and a shabby pair of jeans for yard work.

With a thudding heart she made her way to the dining room.

"Ah. Good morning, Ann. How did you sleep?" Ian set down his newspaper and labored to his feet.

"Good morning, doctor. I slept well." She smiled at his courtly manners and tried not to show the disappointment she felt as her gaze swept the dining room. It was empty except for the elderly scientist. "In fact, I overslept. I'm usually awake at dawn."

Mala shuffled in carrying a tray heaped with toast and eggs. Placing the steaming plates before them she clucked like a mother hen. "Jamie didn't even have time to eat a thing, and already they're bothering him about some ailing cattle. Dr. McFarland, that boy's going to make himself sick.''

Ann nearly choked. That "boy" was the healthiest specimen of a man she had ever seen.

Mala piled Ann's plate with a mound of scrambled eggs, plump sausages, freshly baked bread that had been lightly toasted and a healthy scoop of fresh island fruit preserves.

When Ann tried to protest, Mala commanded, "Eat," as if she were addressing her granddaughter.

Ann tasted, then began smiling as she savored Mala's cooking. Her hurried breakfasts in Boston never seemed as luxurious as this. She was still eating when Jay sauntered into the room, wearing frayed shorts and a faded, open-necked shirt. Bronzed and muscular, he exuded energy and male virility. Ann tried not to stare at the furring of dark hair on his legs. Instead, her gaze strayed to the hair curling on his chest, exposed by the open-necked shirt.

His quick look took in her flushed features and he bestowed a brief smile on her before addressing his father.

"Sorry, Dad. We won't have time for that visit I promised you earlier this morning. I was looking forward to it, but I'll have to drive to the west range. It's something Kai can't handle by himself."

The older man's eyes lit with understanding. "Aye, it's the kind of dedication I understand completely, Jamie. A man's got to see to his responsibilities. We'll talk later."

Jay patted his father on the shoulder. His eyes met Ann's, and for a moment she felt as she had the night before, when he kissed her. Heat coursed through her limbs, staining her cheeks. Her cup clattered against the saucer as her hand trembled. With a curt nod he was gone.

Ann watched the older man's face as Ian's gaze followed his son's progress through the doorway. Gone now was the understanding smile. Instead, she could read a hint of disappointment and, she thought, loneliness. When he turned back to her he had composed himself, offering her a steady smile.

"That lad," he said, shaking his head, "has far too many obligations. I get dizzy trying to keep up with him. He never has time to relax."

Annoyed, Ann kept her thoughts to herself. There was no sense adding to this kind old man's burdens. Yet it didn't seem fair for Jay to spend so much time away from home. He had said he had an assistant. That ought to free him to spend time with his father—if that was what he really wanted. But it could be that he simply wanted to avoid spending time with the frail, elderly man. The thought rankled.

Breaking into her thoughts Ian asked, "Would you like to read a few more of the papers I've been compiling, Ann? They're in my study."

She gave him her warmest smile, hoping to ease the loss of his son's company for at least a little while. "There's nothing I'd like better, Dr. McFarland."

"Good." He offered her his free arm as if he were

gallantly leading her to a dance floor. "I assure you, you'll have my undivided attention."

Ann sat crosslegged on the warm tiles of the patio, wire-rimmed glasses perched on her nose, her head bent over the pages of a report on the exotic birds of the rain forest.

The doctor was ensconced in a wicker settee, his legs stretched out, his cane forgotten on the floor beside him.

After several hours in his study they had moved to this sun-warmed haven, where Mala had served them a magnificent lunch: freshly caught fish, broiled and lightly seasoned, and a salad. Sipping iced tea, Ann turned the page and glanced at the lionine head, tipped back in repose, glinting in the sunlight. With his face to the sky he looked relaxed, younger. Distracted, Ann found herself searching his features for similarities to his son.

"You have a fine mind, Ann." His eyes remained closed. "I've been enjoying our discussion."

She chuckled and felt his sharp blue gaze suddenly focus on her. "That's a polite term for it—a discussion. I'm glad you didn't call it an argument."

"When two scientists have a difference of opinion about an experiment, it's called a discussion. When two scientists decide to discuss world affairs, that's an argument."

They both laughed.

Ann locked her arms around her knees and hugged them closer, regarding Ian warmly. Her voice lowered. "I've enjoyed talking with you, Dr. McFarland." The warmth was evident in her tone. "This day has been a wonderful treat to me."

"Ann, I don't think you know what this has meant to me. I miss this. My children . . ." He looked up at the shadow in the doorway. "Yes, Mala?"

"You have visitors just coming in, doctor."

In the foyer, Laela's voice could be heard, raised in excitement. A moment later, a tall, stunningly beautiful woman swooped through the doorway and hurried to Dr. McFarland's arms.

"Dad."

His arms came around her in a great bear hug. "Janet. What a wonderful surprise. Is Colin with you?"

"Yes. On the spur of the moment we decided to make a celebration of tonight, before Jamie leaves for the month."

She smoothed his brow, then asked, "And where is my favorite brother?"

"On the west range. Seeing to sick cows." His gaze lingered for long moments on the young woman. Then, remembering his manners, the old man said, "Janet, this is our guest, Dr. Ann Lowry. Ann, my daughter, Dr. Janet Wilcox."

Ann stood hastily, brushing her skirt down, and extended her hand. She found herself looking into blue eyes that reminded her of both Ian's and Jay's. The woman's thick auburn hair was pulled back in a comb studded with irridescent shells. She wore a simple blue sheath of watered silk.

"Hello, Dr. Wilcox."

"It's Janet." The other woman smiled. "And you are Dad's guest for the month, doctor?"

Ann nodded. "Please call me Ann." She felt small and plain beside this elegant creature. "What sort of doctor are you, Janet?"

"A pediatrician. My husband Colin and I have a practice on the big island." She turned to a man standing just inside the doorway. "Colin, come meet Dad's guest."

With an affectionate smile, Colin Wilcox shook Ian's hand, insisting that he remain seated. Turning to Ann, he took her hand in his and greeted her warmly.

"Nice to meet you, Ann. I understand you're a botanist. Has Ian been boring you with his slides of the exotic plants of the rain forest?"

Ann thought Janet and Colin Wilcox were the handsomest couple she had ever seen. They were both tall and slim, in their early thirties and her red-brown hair and blue eyes complemented his sandy hair and piercing dark eyes. Colin had casually dropped his arm about his wife's shoulders as he spoke.

"There's no way Dr. McFarland could ever be boring. I'm fascinated with his knowledge. In fact, I've been hanging on his every word." Ann turned. "But you never told me you had slides of plant life, doctor. I'd love to see them."

"Oh, you will. I intended to get around to showing them to you before the day was over."

He stood and Janet was immediately at his side. "Jamie will be so pleased to see both of you," Ian said. "We've missed you." As he moved slowly toward the doorway he added, "But I certainly hope he gets back here in time for dinner." His voice warmed. "You know how that goes."

Janet and Colin exchanged smiles. Nodding, Janet remarked, "We certainly do, Dad. Do you have any idea how difficult it is to leave, even for just a few days?" She caught her father's arm and moved slowly by his side, chatting as they walked. "Colin and I had to check our surgical schedules to be certain we could both be gone. Then we had to locate two doctors who would agree to take any emergency calls for us." With a dry smile she added, "Every child under the age of fifteen who lives within twenty miles of our office will probably come down with a mysterious fever while we're gone. It never fails."

Colin Wilcox walked beside Ann as the four moved to the living room.

"Excited about going into the rain forest, Ann?"

She nodded. "I've read all I could get my hands on. I have several experiments I want to try. And I've brought as much camera equipment as I thought I could safely carry."

"Sounds as though you'll be busy."

"Oh yes. I may never get an opportunity like this again. I have to make every minute count."

Colin glanced down at the intense woman beside him. Her eyes burned with an inner light. He found himself smiling, recalling his days as a young intern.

Ian McFarland settled himself comfortably on the sofa with his daughter beside him. Colin moved to the bar and began to fix drinks.

"What will you have, Ann?" he asked.

"Scotch and soda," Dr. McFarland answered for her as if she had been his guest for years, instead of merely one day.

She found it a pleasant feeling, to be included so easily in the family gathering. Sitting quietly, listening to the doctor and his daughter and son-in-law catch up on the latest news, she found herself wondering idly what it would be like to belong to a busy, interesting family like theirs.

"The dress you're wearing, Janet." Ann paused, slightly embarrassed to admit she knew so little about clothes. "Is it Hawaiian?"

Janet smiled gently, noting Ann's plain dark skirt and prim blouse. "Yes. I found it in a little boutique in Oahu. Maybe before you leave Hawaii we could shop together."

"I'd love that. I'm afraid I have no knack for shopping," Ann admitted.

"Then it's a date," Janet said firmly. "It would be a crime to leave the islands without something to take home that will forever remind you of your visit."

The afternoon passed pleasantly, and Ann found herself impressed with Janet and Colin Wilcox. Despite their hectic schedule, maintaining both a large pediatric practice and serving as surgeons at a nearby hospital, they were devoted to each other and managed to find time to visit the McFarland island whenever they could steal a few days.

By the time they had made their way upstairs to freshen up before dinner, Jay had still not put in an appearance. Ann knew that Dr. McFarland was concerned that Jay wouldn't get home in time to see his sister before leaving in the morning for the field trip.

"Oh Mala." Janet sighed in delight. "I'd forgotten what magic you make in the kitchen. This is wonderful."

Ann glanced across the table at the beautiful woman who had admitted to being Jay's baby sister. At thirty-one, she was two years younger than he, and had jokingly said that she had been playing matchmaker for a number of years, to no avail.

"Doc Jamie's home! Doc Jamie!" At Laela's childish shriek, all heads turned toward the doorway.

A streak of color hurled itself into Jay's arms, shouting, "Doc Janet's here to visit. Look what she brought me."

Everyone watched as Laela hugged him then, stepping away, twirled for Jay's inspection, wearing a pair of bright pink shorts and a shirt that sported every color of island flowers.

"Very pretty, Shrimp."

Ann's gaze swept over the figure in the frayed shorts and dirt-stained shirt. For a moment he seemed fatigued. Then, in an almost effortless gesture, he dismissed it. Despite his wide smile at Laela's display of enthusiasm Ann noted his lazy, almost rougish stance.

He walked to his sister's side and bent to kiss her before shaking Colin's hand.

"We fly all this way to give you a bon voyage party before you go off to the wilds, and this is how you thank us. By staying away all day.'' Janet chuckled. ''It's a good thing Dad was here to greet me, or I would have felt slighted.''

''Sorry, Jan,'' he mumbled, rubbing his hand over his beard. Including the others in his comments, he glanced around, holding Ann's gaze for a long moment. ''Go ahead and eat. I already ate with the Calabash family. I'll just take a few minutes to clean up.''

As he left the room Laela clutched at his arm, chattering like a magpie.

''Wait till you see the dress Doc Janet brought me. It's almost as beautiful as the one you bought for my birthday.''

As her voice faded, Janet exchanged a smile with her husband seated across the table. ''Poor Jamie. She'll talk his arm off until he closes his door.''

Colin winked. ''He doesn't mind in the least. Your brother enjoys that chatterbox.''

While the others finished their dinner Ann picked at her food. She had suddenly lost her appetite. It was not, she told herself firmly, because of Jay McFarland. It was simply the excitement of the approaching trip.

After a dessert of fresh fruit and ice cream, they left the dining room and moved to a long veranda overlooking the rolling hills that led to the waters of the channel. On a coffee table Mala set a tray laden with a silver coffee service. Colin mixed drinks at a small bar. Relaxed, content, they stretched out on comfortable wicker chaises.

Although she was listening intently to something Ian

was saying, Ann knew the exact moment Jay entered the room. Without realizing it, her senses had been tuned to him. She turned her head, watching as he moved toward them. He was wearing dark slacks and a pale, open-neck shirt. Droplets of water from the shower still glistened in his shaggy hair.

With a careless gesture, he dropped his arm around his sister's waist, and she leaned against him. It was obvious that she adored him.

Colin handed him a drink, and Jay smiled his appreciation.

"Long day, Jamie? You look a bit tired."

Jay took a long pull on the drink before casually dismissing the question. "Just another day of fun in the sun. Who's covering your practice while you two play?"

Janet pulled his beard. "We will owe two doctors our very souls when we get back. It took some doing to get them to cover for us." She laughed as he pulled his chin away. "You're starting to look like some wild mountain man, Jamie dear. I wish some woman would take you in hand and civilize you."

"And make me give up this devil-may-care lifestyle, my dear? Not on your stethoscope. I've found it's easier to just drift through life alone."

"Lazy," she retorted before turning to sit on the arm of her father's chair.

Ann had watched the exchange in silence. It was obvious to her that Jay had indeed given up on civilization. He preferred long hours in the sun to disciplined work schedules.

"This was quite a surprise, having Janet and Colin drop by. Don't you agree, Jamie?" Ian said with obvious enthusiasm.

"It's great, Dad. I'm only sorry we can't have more time to visit. You two went to a lot of trouble for so little time."

"We thought we'd stay on for another week and have a nice long visit with Dad."

Jay studied his sister for a long moment. "That's great. Dad's missed you."

"He's grown accustomed to missing his children, haven't you, Dad?" Janet kissed his cheek.

"Absolutely. And I may never forgive either of you for being so busy and successful." Ann realized there was no rancor in Ian's voice. He was merely teasing, even if it were a fact of life.

While the teasing banter went on among the family members, Ann was content to watch and listen. It was a bright, intensely alive group, everyone with a genuine affection for each other. Yet several times while the others were talking she sensed that Jay had withdrawn mentally. He seemed distracted and appeared to have to force himself to join in the conversation.

She was surprised when he drew a chair near hers and sat down.

"Did you and my father have a good visit?"

She tensed, wishing he hadn't pulled his chair so near.

"Yes. He's a fascinating man. The hours flew by while we talked about his experiments and the papers he's written. I had a wonderful day. You would have enjoyed yourself if you had stayed."

His eyes scanned her features while she spoke. "Why do I get the feeling you're accusing me?"

She flushed.

"I don't know what you mean."

Through narrowed lids he watched her a moment longer, before forcing his attention back to the conversation of his sister and her husband.

Ian McFarland was the first to retire for the night. He rose stiffly, leaning heavily on his cane, and kissed his daughter with great tenderness before bidding goodnight to the others. The smile he bestowed on his son was filled with affection.

For a long while after he left, Jay and Janet spoke of their father, discussing his health. Ann realized while they talked that Janet and Colin actually intended to stay on so that they could closely observe her father, in order to determine that he was getting as much medical attention as he needed.

It was nearly midnight when Janet smiled gently at her husband.

"Your eyes are practically closing while we talk. Come on, darling. It's time for bed."

He turned apologetically to Jay. "Sorry to drop out without more time for talk, Jamie, but it's been a long day. If we miss your departure in the morning, take care." They shook hands. "We'll spend as much time with your dad as we can before we leave."

"Thanks, Colin." Jay bent to kiss his sister's cheek. "I'm glad you came. Sorry it's so brief a visit."

She hugged him. "The story of our life, isn't it?"

Turning to Ann, she smiled. "It's been good meeting you, Ann. I hope your research in the rain forest goes well."

Ann stood, placing her glass on the table. She didn't want to be left alone with Jay. Intent on following the others from the room she was startled when Jay stopped her.

His hand on her arm was warm. When she turned, the midnight blue of his eyes held her gaze.

"Are you tired, Ann?"

"Yes." She tried to keep the edge from her voice.

"Odd. You didn't seem the least bit tired a few minutes ago." She hated the way he studied her, like a moth under a microscope.

"It's been a long day for some of us." She tried to turn away, but his firm grip stopped her.

"I've been watching those little flames dart into your eyes ever since I entered the room. You've been itching for a fight all night, Ann. Out with it."

She backed away but Jay's hands caught her shoulders, holding her firmly.

After a lifetime of practice, Ann was able to keep a tight leash on her temper. Control. It was a discipline she had learned at an early age. But Jay's touch and the nearness of him were overpowering. Her control slipped.

"All right." She expelled an angry breath. "I happen to think your father's a very nice, very special man."

He studied her face carefully. "Is that supposed to be profound?"

She jerked herself free of his hold and half turned,

avoiding his eyes. "I just mean that Ian's too nice to be hurt like this. You had no right to leave him alone on your last day at home. He was looking forward to being with you. I was a poor substitute."

His voice was so near, she shivered. "I was looking forward to the pleasure of his company as well. What is this leading to?"

At her prolonged silence he said, in an ominously quiet voice, "Let's have it, Ann."

She turned and met his questioning look. "You calmly saunter in here after a day at the beach, to say you've already had your dinner with the . . . Calabashes, and expect him to accept your snub without question."

She could see the red beard twitch as the merest hint of a smile touched his lips. The laugh reached his eyes, creating fine lines in his bronzed skin.

He threw back his head in a roar of laughter, then caught her by the shoulders, drawing her closer. For a moment longer the laugh continued, then he sobered and stared down into her upturned face.

"In Hawaiian, the calabash family is the extended family—all those who have shared your joys and sorrows. They can be friends, neighbors. The calabash is a common bowl—shared by those who care." He added with a twinkle, "After I finished my business on the west range I was expected to eat with my friends."

He watched the flush of color that swept from her throat to her cheeks. "I thought—you had deliberately ignored your father, because you wanted to relax."

His voice took on a deeper timbre. "Now I understand. With that very proper little skirt and blouse and your hair all bound up tightly to your head, you do look like the missionaries who came over here to convert the heathens.'' He gave her a mocking smile. "So you've decided to convert this sinful, prodigal son, have you, little Annie?''

She flushed and glanced down at her hands clenched tightly in front of her, as if to create a barrier between them.

He tipped up her chin. "Do you think you can convert a sinner like me?''

She licked her lips before answering. "Do you need converting?'' She found her gaze drawn to his mouth, just inches above hers. She caught her breath at the thought of those lips on hers.

"Ah, but what if the sinner converts the saint instead?'' He chuckled, and the sound of it slid across her nerves, causing a sensation low in her spine.

"I would suppose, Jay, that living here on this island would tend to make you . . . careless. Careless of schedules. Careless of people's feelings. Maybe even careless of simple moral principles.'' She tore her gaze from his tantalizing mouth and met his eyes. "But just because I do care, that doesn't make me a . . . missionary, or a saint.'' She tried to draw back. "And I still think you're the type of man who does exactly as he pleases, regardless of what others think.''

"You're right, little Annie. And what I please is this.''

With his hands on her shoulders he drew her tightly to him, until she was nearly lifted on tiptoe. Her eyes rounded in surprise. The lips that took hers held none of the tenderness of the previous night. There was a hint of anger in his kiss, as well as possession. When she stiffened, his arms came around her, drawing her against him until she was aware of the entire length of him. The kiss was hot, demanding. Shock waves rippled through her.

He lifted his lips a little, allowing them to brush hers softly. Against her mouth he said, "Now it's your turn, little missionary. Would you like to kiss me back?"

"Don't be—" Her words were cut off by the slightest pressure of his lips on hers.

Still, he hesitated, lifting his lips until they hovered just above hers, tempting, tantalizing.

Her hands tentatively touched his waist. There was a weakness spreading through her limbs, and she had a terrible need to cling to him.

"Jay, I . . ."

"It won't hurt, Ann. Just kiss me."

With a sigh she drew him closer, pressing her lips to his. She felt his sudden intake of breath as he wrapped her in an embrace that seemed to envelop her in exploding passion.

Ann felt lost in the wonder of these new feelings. Never before had she wanted to give, to take, to experience such emotions. Her lips opened to him, allowing him to explore her mouth while she tasted him with a new hunger.

Her gradual surrender only fueled his passion. The hands that held her tightly now began to move slowly over her body, drawing her hips tightly to him.

She wound her arms around his neck, then allowed

herself the luxury of touching his shaggy hair and beard. A soft moan escaped her lips.

His hands roamed upwards, encircling her small waist, then moving up to trace her ribs and the roundness of her breasts. His thumbs brushed across the softness beneath the prim blouse.

Shocked, she tried to pull away, but his arms drew her firmly against him. She had never before allowed a man to touch her like this. But Jay McFarland was like no man she had ever met. The hands that moved along her back were gentle now, coaxing her to relax once more against him.

"Oh, little Annie," he muttered against her cheek. "I'm going to enjoy being converted. You have such zeal. And even if you fail, and I succeed in converting you to my sinful, lazy ways instead, think of the fun it will be."

His lips took hers again, slowly, seductively, as if proving they had all the time in the world. Wrapped in a hazy glow, Ann allowed herself to enjoy the touch of his lips on hers, feeling the heat of his body engulfing hers in fire.

When at last he lifted his lips, he continued to hold her, staring down into her eyes.

"The rain forest is like another world," he murmured, pressing his lips to her temple. "There will be only the two of us. Hidden behind a veil of mist, in a lush paradise, I'll introduce you to all life's secrets."

He studied her face, noting the crimson staining her cheeks and throat. Her skin felt as if it were on fire.

She searched her inner being for the control she had

always been able to count on. Slowly, she felt her mind clearing, her sanity returning. This had been just a moment of madness. Now, before it went any further, she had to set him straight.

"I don't make it a habit to go around kissing . . . barbarians. And I certainly don't need you to introduce me to any of life's secrets. I'm a scientist, in case you've forgotten. And an intelligent person. What you'll be in the rain forest is my guide. Nothing more." Her eyes darkened to gold, flecked with brown. "Is that understood?"

He smiled, a lazy, almost wicked smile that made her want to slap his arrogant face.

"I understand a lot more than you think, little Annie Laurie. And I think I'm going to enjoy the next month with you." He paused, studying the smoldering fire in her eyes. "A paragon of virtue, and a barbarian. In other words, a saint and a sinner. Interesting." He traced her lips with his fingertip and felt her stiffen suddenly. "Very interesting."

She turned and strode from the room, fleeing up the stairs, feeling his gaze burning into her. She wouldn't look back. She wouldn't give him the satisfaction. Besides, she was certain he was still smiling.

Chapter Four

The sun had not yet risen, but the first pale fingers of light streaked the distant horizon. The morning's cheerful bird chorus hadn't yet begun. Even the constant sounds of the island—the buzzing of insects, gentle breezes rustling the palms outside the balcony—seemed to have stilled.

For one brief moment Ann snuggled into the softness of the bed, allowing herself the luxury of savoring the thought of Jay's kiss. His touch affected her as no one else's ever had. It bothered her that he had managed to insinuate himself into her orderly life. She seemed to be spending more time thinking about him than she spent on the reason for this trip.

She mentally shook herself. Her thoughts were totally unprofessional. An idle mind was the devil's workshop.

From now on she would keep herself too busy to think about Jay McFarland.

With a concerted effort Ann bounded from the bed. She opened the drapes and stared at the paradise spread out below her. The rich colors were muted in the dawn haze to the soft shades of a surrealistic watercolor. The land was in slumber, as if waiting for her to coax it awake. She felt intensely alive. This day would begin a journey that for her was the culmination of years of struggle, study and preparation. Now she could set aside the dull routine of the classroom and immerse herself in the one thing that stirred her passion—field research.

Eager to start the day, she bathed and dressed in a pair of heavy khaki pants and a long-sleeved shirt. Carefully tucking her pant legs deep inside tall army-style hiking boots, she tied the laces tightly. Her hair was slicked back in a severe knot. Over this she tied a cotton bandana.

With meticulous care, Ann laid out the supplies she had brought for the trip. As each item was packed she checked it off, until at last the list was completed. Satisfied, Ann studied the pack, which contained a change of clothing and underthings, gym shoes, her camera and photographic accessories, notepads, pens, a portable tape recorder and a one-man tent, along with a number of necessary toiletries.

She carefully rolled and secured the canvas. Slipping both arms through the handles, she hefted the pack upward to her shoulders. The extreme weight of the load knocked her off balance. She stumbled backward, landing like a turtle on her back on the bed.

For one startled moment she lay on top of the mountain of equipment, her feet kicking helplessly, her mouth opened in surprise. Angrily she slipped her arms from the straps. Free of the restraint, she dropped to the floor. Kicking the bed in silent fury, she pondered what to do. She had to lighten her load, and yet everything she had packed was necessary.

How would she ever manage all this? She frowned. The answer was simple. Jay. Though she hated to owe him a favor she would ask him to help her carry her gear. After all, that giant of a man could at least make himself useful.

She hauled the heavy load to the door, sliding it across the floor by one handle. When she reached the stairs, she gritted her teeth, tugged with all her might and managed to move it downstairs step-by-step.

From one of the many pockets of her khaki shirt she removed a plastic pouch and headed for the kitchen.

"What in the world . . . ?"

Ann stopped in midstride to stare in disbelief at Jay, dressed as always in cut-offs and a flowery shirt, his feet bare, eating the biggest bowl of chocolate ice cream she had ever seen. There must have been nearly a quart mounded in the enormous bowl. On his face was a look of pure delight.

"Want some?" He held out the spoon.

"Don't be ridiculous." Ann looked thunderstruck before turning away to search the cupboards for a bowl.

Jay studied her rigid back and allowed his gaze to roam slowly over her. "Dressed for jungle warfare, I see." The warmth of laughter colored his tone.

She ignored him. His sarcasm didn't deserve a response.

Locating a bowl, she dumped in the contents of the plastic pouch. Over that she poured some milk. Taking the seat across the table from Jay, she began to mechanically eat her breakfast.

"What is that stuff?" Jay eyed it as if it were poison.

"It's a special blend of dried fruit, seeds, nuts and whole grains, fortified with wheat germ and high protein. Mountaineers and hikers always eat it for energy."

"It looks like sawdust mixed with a few things nice people wouldn't dream of putting in their mouths. Why don't you have some bacon and eggs?"

"For your information, this is very nutritious. It contains more protein than a steak."

"But I bet it's no fun to eat. Annie, try a little of my ice cream."

She glowered at him as if he had just asked her to commit a crime. "I can't believe a grown man would actually eat chocolate ice cream for breakfast."

"Is there some rule that says we can only enjoy good things after a certain hour?" He pinned her with those blue eyes. "Are you one of those people who believes in a time for everything?" His eyes glinted with humor. "I'll bet you even believe couples should only make love after dark, with the lights out and the curtains drawn."

"Must everything you say or do have a sexual connotation?" She looked as if she had just eaten a prune, and continued her meal in silence.

He took another spoonful of ice cream and sighed. "Do you realize I won't get another chance to eat this for a month? A whole month." He grinned wickedly, raising one eyebrow as if he had just had a deliciously evil thought. "So, little Annie, you eat your sawdust. I want you full of energy." He chuckled, and she realized his laughter was a lovely sound even if his insinuations were obvious. "But as for me—I'll enjoy this sinful dessert."

She shook her head at his childish behavior and finished her breakfast without comment. There was no sense putting up a fight. He was determined to tease her without mercy.

While she ate she felt his gaze burn slowly over her. "By the way, just why are you wearing those army fatigues?" he asked dryly.

"Dr. Smythe-Fielding recommended these."

"Really. Did he say why?"

"For protection from insect bites, extreme moisture, whatever else I may encounter in the rain forest. I suppose if it's good enough for our soldiers, it's good enough for me."

The red beard twitched, as if he found her comments amusing. "I'm sure Dr. Smythe-Fielding is an expert." In an undertone, he added, "After all, I'm only the lowly guide." He glanced up to meet her steady gaze. "But all that military gear is really unnecessary, Ann."

She shrugged. "As you said. Dr. Smythe-Fielding is an expert."

When she had rinsed her dishes and loaded them in the dishwasher, she turned. "Have you packed your gear yet?"

Jay licked the spoon. "What gear? I'm only the guide, remember?"

She felt exasperated at his endless teasing. "But you must need a few things. We're going to be gone a month."

"Um-hmm."

For a moment she thought he was actually going to lick the bowl. Instead he stood, towering over her, and rinsed his dishes before placing them beside hers in the dishwasher.

"Jay, aren't you bringing anything along in the rain forest?"

"A few things. I prefer to travel light."

She smiled. "In that case then, I hope you won't mind helping me with some of my gear."

He shot her a suspicious look. "That depends."

"On what?"

"On how much gear you're talking about."

She dried her hands and led the way to the foyer, where her pack loomed even larger than she remembered.

"I'm having a little trouble carrying all this. If I divided it into two packs, do you think you could carry one?"

He stood, hands on hips, regarding her with disbelief. "You can't be serious. Why would you haul all this stuff with you?"

"I checked my list very carefully. Everything in this pack is necessary, Jay."

"We'll see about that." He knelt and began unrolling

the canvas. As Ann seethed in anger he began sorting through her belongings, setting them in two piles.

When he reached her underthings and picked up a pair of sheer bikini panties, she reached the boiling point.

"Why Miss Prim and Proper Ann Lowry. Do you mean that beneath those army fatigues you're actually wearing some feminine doodads?"

"Give me those!" Snatching them from his hands, she grabbed up a lacy nude-colored bra as well and turned away in anger, nearly bumping into Ian McFarland.

"Well." His gaze skimmed the items clutched in Ann's hand. He noted the dark look on her face and cleared his throat. "Packing, Ann?"

She held her hands behind her back and refused to meet his direct gaze. "Yes. Good morning, Dr. McFarland."

"Actually, we're unpacking, Dad," came Jay's gruff voice from the floor. "Ann decided to carry all the trappings of civilization into the jungle. Right now I'm searching for her hidden television set."

The doctor coughed discreetly. "I'm so glad I had the chance to see you before you left. Why don't you both join me for coffee before you start off on your journey?"

His son's head tipped up, and Ian saw the gleam of mischief in his eyes.

Jay stood. "Good idea, Dad. Ann, you join my father. I'll be there in just a minute."

"But my . . ."

"I'll take care of everything. Go ahead."

Before she could protest Dr. McFarland's hand was

beneath her elbow, guiding her toward the dining room. The items still held in her hand were quickly stuffed into one of the pockets of her khaki shirt. To her consternation, she heard footsteps on the stairs and turned to see Janet and Colin descending toward them.

"Ah. Good. We've all managed to wake up before your departure." Dr. McFarland's face was wreathed in smiles. "Janet. Colin. Join us for breakfast. We'll have a fine sendoff for the two travelers."

Ann wanted to groan with impatience. Instead, forcing a cheerfulness she didn't feel, she smiled a greeting.

Janet hugged her father and the two of them preceded Ann and Colin into the dining room.

Colin studied the tense young woman beside him. "I suppose it must be quite different, coming from a regulated academic life in Boston to this offbeat island. But Ann, if you begin to realize that schedules have no place in this part of the world, maybe you can begin to relax and actually enjoy this experience."

She smiled her gratitude. "Is my impatience so obvious, Colin?"

He gave her a gentle smile. "Your face, and especially those big eyes of yours are quite expressive."

She flushed, remembering Jay's words.

Colin spoke softly to ease her discomfort. "We're a bit off the beaten path here, Ann. And in order to survive we've become adaptable. But it takes time. You're still running on alarm clocks, and schedules and traffic jams. If you stayed around long enough, you'd forget what those things are."

"I can't imagine not having to live on a schedule. It's

my lifeblood. I'm one of those people who thrives on lists of chores. I take a great deal of satisfaction in working my way through long lists of things to do.'' She glanced at him as he held her chair. ''Does that sound very strange, Colin?''

He smiled as he shook his head. ''Not at all, Ann. In fact, I seem to remember a young intern who felt much the same way.''

At his wry smile, his wife chuckled and added, ''Ann, my husband actually had the beginnings of an ulcer when he came to Hawaii. The laidback man you see before you is very different from the uptight doctor I first met.''

Jay entered the room in time to hear the last of the conversation. Pulling out a chair beside Ann he muttered, ''Well then, I suppose there's still room for hope.''

''Hope for whom?'' Ann regarded him with a cool glare.

He shrugged.

''Did you divide my gear into two packs?''

''Yes. We'll manage.''

Ann groaned as Mala entered bearing trays of steaming eggs, fat sausages, mounds of potatoes plus an overflowing plate of island fruit.

''We won't be able to walk half a mile after packing away all this food.''

Jay winked at her and Ann felt her heart tumble wildly in her chest. ''Stop worrying, little Annie. The world won't come to an end if you indulge yourself. Enjoy this last civilized meal.''

To her surprise the meal was a pleasure. The conversation between Dr. McFarland and his family was stimulating, and at times silly. Sitting back, sipping strong hot coffee, Ann realized just how much these people enjoyed each other's company. She had not had the opportunity to be part of a family for a long time, but she thought they were more in tune with each other's needs than most people she knew.

At long last the leisurely meal drew to a close, and Jay signaled an end to breakfast by pushing away from the table. He held Ann's chair, then dropped a kiss on his sister's cheek.

"Hold the fort, Janet."

Janet stood and hugged him, then turned to Ann. "Don't let him drift too far from civilized ways, Ann. He's already become too much of a barbarian. Good luck in your research."

"Thank you."

Ann watched as Jay and his father caught each other in a great bear hug.

With a smile, Dr. McFarland bent to kiss her cheek. "Just relax and make this the experience of a lifetime, Ann. I know you're in no danger with Jay along."

Ann wondered if the elderly doctor knew what he was saying. Probably her greatest danger lay in the fact that Jay would be along. Jay—and no one else.

After a brief kiss from Colin, Ann hurried after the figure of Jay, already striding from the room.

Outside, their packs had been stored in the back of a jeep.

She paused. "I'll be right back." Ann hurried upstairs, where she reached a hand inside her pocket, retrieved her underthings and jammed them into a drawer. They were the only items she could actually do without. And for the sake of practicality she was willing to leave them behind. With a last reluctant glance at the luxurious room she hurried to the idling jeep.

With a simple shifting of gears they left the big house behind and began driving to the center of the island of Kalai. It might as well have been to the end of the earth. Civilization and all its rules would be left behind.

During the long drive, Jay explained a few facts about the island's rain forest.

"This is our winter season. The Kona winds carry rain and humid weather across the Pacific. But here on Kalai the tallest mountain peak in the area attracts rain clouds like a magnet. We've measured more than forty feet of rainfall in a single year in the forest, making it one of the rainiest spots on earth. The water constantly scours the canyons with runoff. You'll see some of the most spectacular waterfalls anywhere in the world right here on this trip, Ann."

She felt her heartbeat quicken. Far ahead she could already see the peak of the mountain, wreathed by gauzy clouds.

As they drew nearer her voice lowered. "I feel so lucky to be able to go on this field trip, Jay. Do you know what it means to me?" She turned her head, meeting his blue gaze. "This is the chance of a lifetime for a scientist."

"Dad believes you're one of the best."

She flushed. This was high praise, coming from a man who would never offer empty flattery.

His voice took on a sterner edge. "One rule. While we're in the rain forest, you have to take orders from me."

Seeing her mouth move in a protest, he interrupted, "No room for argument, Ann. While we're here, I'm not only your guide, I'm in charge. There can be only one boss, and I'm it." He held her gaze. "I'm responsible for your safety. I make all the rules. Understood?"

Her lips tightened to a thin line. He left her no choice. With obvious anger she nodded her agreement.

"Good."

As they drew nearer Ann could make out the fine veil of mist ahead, marking the beginning of the rain forest.

"What will you do with the jeep?"

"I'll just leave it at the edge of the forest, with the keys in the ignition, in case of an emergency. Anyone who comes across it will understand why it's here. If they need it they can use it and then return it."

Ann shook her head in wonder. "You're talking to someone who can't even work in her back yard without locking the front door. I wouldn't dream of leaving my car parked in front of my house with the keys inside. It wouldn't last an hour."

"That's the joy of owning your own island." He turned smiling eyes to her. "Where would a thief be able to take a stolen jeep on this island?"

She joined his laughter. "That's a good point."

He turned off the ignition. Following his lead Ann

stepped from the jeep and lifted a pack. She was surprised at how light it felt.

"What did you take out?"

He grinned. "I have all your camera gear in my pack, since that was the heaviest."

She adjusted the pack, then took a few tentative steps. "But this is so light. Do you have my tent too?"

He nodded, adjusting the larger pack across his shoulders.

He met her gaze, noting the excitement dancing in her wide, amber eyes.

"Ready, Ann?"

"Oh yes."

They stepped from brilliant sunshine and a typically balmy Hawaiian day into the muted light of the rain forest. The carpet beneath their feet was thick with moss and lush vegetation. The rain wasn't really a heavy rainfall, but rather a fine mist that felt warm, almost steamy against their skin.

Ann lifted her face to the thick canopy of vines overhead. Instead of the dark, gloomy forest she'd expected, she was amazed to note that even in the most thickly shadowed glade there was a marvelous luminescence, an amber-green light that bathed everything in its glow.

Her voice was hushed. "Oh Jay. Look at this strange radiance. Is it always like this?"

He turned, and she noted that his voice was softer too. "Yes. Isn't it fascinating?" He lifted a finger to her eyelashes, matted with moisture. "When I was a little boy I thought this place was touched by magic."

Her voice was barely a whisper. "I think it is."

He stared at her a long time, then turned and once again took the lead.

Brilliantly colored birds, which to Ann's trained eye were rare and probably never seen outside this perimeter, darted from tree to tree, some warbling the sweetest notes she had ever heard.

Her mind, like a computer, began sorting out the various plant life, assimilating information, cataloging and always searching for the rare or—even more important—the never-before-seen plant or flower.

"Will you set up a base camp?" she asked. It annoyed her that she had to speak to his back, which always seemed to be a dozen paces ahead of her. She was struggling to keep up with his long strides.

He turned and, seeing her predicament, paused until she was directly beside him. "No. Everything is portable. We'll just carry the equipment with us each day. That way, if you find something you want to explore further, we won't have to leave it and return to a camp."

"Oh, that's wonderful. I thought we'd have to work our way each day from a certain point." She smiled. "Will we really get to investigate every part of the forest before we return?"

"Why not? That's what you came for, isn't it? I'd hate to think you had to go back to Boston without seeing everything we had to offer."

He started walking again, but she noted that his strides were shorter, less hurried. He was allowing her to keep up without effort.

"There's a place I'd like to show you before it grows

dark." He caught her hand suddenly, as a fallen log blocked their path.

As she was about to cross she stopped suddenly and knelt in the soft moss.

"Look, Jay."

He paused and knelt beside her. "Yes. Seedlings have begun to sprout and grow on the decomposed log. That's the beauty of nature undisturbed. Each time a tree dies it serves as a 'nurse log' for other young trees. By the time this log has completely decomposed, another tree will take its space."

Something in his words triggered a memory. She shook her head, as if to clear her thoughts. "What has gone before charts a course for what will follow." Her voice was a whisper. "Both my parents were scientists. And from my earliest days they planted in me the seed of knowledge. I suppose it's only natural that I wanted to be a scientist too. But until this moment, I never realized that I might be doing it for them."

"Understandable." He frowned. "But it would be better to live your own life, for your own reasons."

He caught her hand and helped her up.

"Is that what you do, Jay?"

He pressed his fingers lightly over her mouth, sending a strange curling sensation along her spine. "You ask too many questions, Annie Laurie. Come on."

Chapter Five

As they tramped along miles of lush forest it was easy to forget that another world existed beyond this. Every inch of space was choked with vine and fern, flowers and plants. The moist air was heady with the perfume of a million rare flowers.

Ann felt that she had entered a strange new fantasy world. Here, time stood still. Bathed in a strange sunlight that filtered through foliage and mist, they moved through a forest whose thick trees formed towering cathedral spires.

Brilliantly colored birds flitted across their path, often blending in so perfectly with the bright array of flowers that they couldn't be detected until they left their perches to become airborne.

As they moved deeper into the forest, Ann found herself completely enchanted with this strange new world. Forgotten for the moment were the experiments she planned, the copious notes she intended to keep. It was enough to be actually walking through the rain forest of Kalai. She felt as if she were treading on sacred ground. It was impossible to hide the note of awe in her tone.

"I hear thunder, Jay."

He turned with a mysterious smile. "That isn't thunder you hear. Look."

He lifted thick, velvety vines, heavy with moisture, as if holding open a door. As Ann moved through the opening in the jungle, she stopped in midstride.

In front of them was a pool of pale green water, made even greener by the glow of the jungle light. On the far side of the pool was a waterfall, cascading from a mountain peak far above them. The sound of the rushing waterfall roared like thunder in the silent forest. High above the treeline the water gleamed molten gold in the sunlight. Beneath the canopy of greenery the golden cascade became an amber green.

"Oh, Jay. It's unbelievably beautiful."

He paused a moment to enjoy the look on her expressive face. "Isn't it lovely? This is one of my favorite spots in the forest. I wanted you to share it." He dropped his pack and lifted the lighter load from her back.

"Would you like to spend the first night here?"

She nodded, suddenly relieved to have come to an end to their walking.

"I'd like that."

"Good. We'll make camp here. I think you've walked

far enough for your first day." He turned with a smile. "Hungry?"

She laughed, and he watched the transformation as her features softened into rare beauty. "Is that all you ever think about? Food?"

He brushed her cheek with the back of his fingers, sending tiny splinters along her spine. "No. Occasionally I think about other, even more pleasant things."

She flushed and turned away, embarrassed by his teasing manner.

"Well. The first thing I'm going to do, even before I think about food—or other things—is jump in that pool." He sat in the wet grass and pulled off his canvas shoes. As he began to unbutton his shirt he added, "And you should do the same, Ann. Those wet clothes must be heavy by now." He stared at her tall hiking boots. "And your feet must feel like they weigh a ton, tramping through the forest in those."

"No. I'm fine."

He glanced up at her and realized that she was once more uncomfortable in his presence. It seemed as if this shyness came over her whenever she realized she was alone with him. It was an oddly guileless, appealing quality about her that made his blood pound in his temples.

He cautioned himself to be patient and respect her sense of propriety. This was going to take a lot more time than he had realized.

"Suit yourself. I'm going swimming." When he stood, Ann picked up her pack and walked to a boulder, where she turned her back and pretended to be busy.

She was horrified by the thought that he was going to undress right here in front of her. She didn't know quite how to deal with this situation. Certainly Jay had the right to swim wherever he pleased. And she was aware that he had probably spent a lifetime swimming with nothing on and felt completely at home doing so here in his rain forest. But this was an entirely alien situation for her. She was trying to behave in an adult fashion. Yet, somehow, this whole state of affairs felt wrong for her.

She waited until she heard the splash of water before turning around. Jay was frolicking in the pool like a seal. He swam underwater the entire length, then came up behind the waterfall, where he called and waved. Moments later he dropped beneath the green water once more, finally surfacing at the opposite side of the pond.

She found herself smiling at his silliness, and yearning for the freedom to join him. It looked like such fun. But she couldn't. She didn't know how to drop her guard and simply be carefree. She had never allowed herself that sort of luxury in her entire life.

For nearly an hour, while Ann made notes in her journal, Jay relaxed in the soothing waters of the pool. She was bent over her notepad, completely lost in her work, when Jay finally walked from the water. It was too late for her to turn away, and she noted with relief that he was wearing his shorts. The wet fabric clung to his hips and thighs like a second skin. As he strode from the pool silver droplets fell from his dark hair. Her gaze roamed over the dark, red-bronze hair matted on his chest.

She tried not to stare at the muscles that rippled across his shoulders and back as he pulled on a fresh shirt.

When he turned to her, her eyes were fixed discreetly on the paper in her lap.

There was the warmth of unspoken laughter in his voice. "All right, Ann. It's your turn."

As she began to protest he added, "Check your watch. I'm going to leave you for an hour."

Seeing her surprised look, he said firmly, "One hour. I promise. In that time, you can swim, bathe, wash your hair, whatever you want, without interruption. I'll go far enough away so you'll have complete privacy. But if there's an emergency, just scream. I'll come running."

At her skeptical look he added, "I give you my word that I won't return for one hour. Starting now."

He picked up his shoes and disappeared into the jungle. With a little laugh of surprise, Ann watched his retreating back until he was out of sight. For long moments she simply stood staring at the wall of foliage around her. Then, realizing what a lovely gift Jay had just given her, she hurriedly dropped her notebook back into the pack and began undressing.

As Jay walked away, the lilting sound of her laughter trailed after him. He realized that he loved that sound. It was delightful, like the sound of a child's innocent laughter.

Innocent. This woman, Ann Lowry, was brilliant, well educated, disciplined—and innocent. There was something rather exciting about that knowledge. Exciting and frustrating.

Jay sat down on a log and slipped on his shoes, then checked his watch. Taking a cigar from his pocket, he lit it, then leaned back against the trunk of a tree and relaxed, watching the wreath of smoke curl upward in the mist-laden air.

She had the most beautiful eyes he had ever seen. Softest amber, they darkened with little brown flecks when she was angry. When she was aroused they glowed like a cat's eyes, round and luminous, glazed with passion.

He could read vulnerability in those eyes. It would be a terrible thing to see her hurt. He felt a fierce protectiveness for her, and the feeling puzzled him. He had always treasured his independence. He had no desire to take on anyone else's problems. Yet something about Ann brought all his male instincts to the surface.

This woman was the kind of challenge any man would enjoy, but especially a man like him. Raised in an intellectual atmosphere, he was accustomed to participating in wide-ranging discussions. He found that he loved the way her mind worked.

He liked listening to her. Though she seldom gave away anything of herself, there were rare times when some little thing slipped out, some tiny bit of information that told him something about her personal life. There was an underlying sadness in her at times, as though she had been deeply hurt in the past. Yet he sensed a basic optimism in her. She believed in herself.

Though he abhorred lists and schedules, he was highly disciplined. He took his work seriously but rarely talked about it. Jay knew that he and Ann appeared to be diametrical opposites. She carried endless lists of jobs she wanted to accomplish. She took herself so seriously that there were times he had to force himself not to laugh at her. It was as if the whole world depended on her knowledge and hard work, and hers alone. Hard work was as essential to her as breathing. She acted as though she could push a button and make herself keep on going, no matter how weary she really felt.

He smiled and watched a smoke ring. She was so damn prim and proper. What fun it would be to muss that neat hair. He wondered what it would look like, falling soft and loose about her face and shoulders instead of being pinned back in that plain bun. It would be sweet torment to unbutton that heavy khaki shirt and find the very feminine body hidden underneath. When he had held her in his arms he'd realized that although she was tiny, she was soft and round in all the right places. She was very much a woman, though she might be trying to deny her womanhood.

She looked fragile, but she was so strong inside. Steel beneath silk. He loved watching her fight to control that fiery temper. What must it be like when she exploded? Fireworks, he decided, taking a long drag on the cigar. The Fourth of July. She kept such a tight lid on that temper, she'd be like a volcano when she finally erupted. Maybe that. was why he so enjoyed teasing her. She always took the bait. And then, when she realized she'd been had, he loved watching her wage that inner battle with her temper. One of these times, he knew, he'd go too far—and he would see just what she would do.

He chuckled at the way his thoughts had rambled. Odd, he mused, this had begun as a favor to his father. But all that had changed when she stepped off that

plane—hot, tired and more than a little frightened. He
had seen all that at once. But she had been like a neatly
wrapped package sent through the mail. Beneath the
plain brown wrapper there had been flashes of brilliant
color, the rustle of tissue paper and the enticing knowledge that a treasure lay just inside the wrappings. He had
to unwrap her, layer by layer, until he found the treasure:
the real Ann Lowry.

Maybe she really believed that she was that cool,
composed iceberg. Jay knew better. From the way she
had responded to him he recognized the simmering
passion that lay just beneath her calm, unruffled surface.
That knowledge tantalized him. He wanted to take her in
his arms and fan those carefully banked coals until they
burst into flame for him. His hand tightened around a
small branch and snapped it off suddenly. If he weren't
careful, this challenge might become an obsession. She
was getting under his skin. This highbrow, uptight,
proper little scientist was like an itch.

He checked his watch and stubbed out his cigar. He
had given her the promised hour. No more. It was time
to get back and set up camp. He grinned. Besides, this
evening promised to be interesting. He might even get to
witness the first real fireworks if her temper erupted the
way he expected it to—when she found out what he had
done with her tent.

Ann was seated on a boulder, feeling deliciously
refreshed. She was dressed in her spare khaki shirt and
pants. The other set had been washed and was spread out
on a low bush.

Her freshly washed hair fell in dripping tendrils around her face and shoulders. Her heavy hiking boots dangled upside down from a tree branch. The only concessions she had made to the steaming jungle were the rolled sleeves of her shirt and the bare feet she wriggled contentedly.

Her glowing, well-scrubbed face was turned up to catch the gentle mist, giving her skin a sheen.

For a minute Jay stood at the edge of the clearing, watching her. It was the first time he had seen her hair loose. It was very long, he realized, falling below her shoulders. Thick and wet, the ends frizzed into little corkscrew curls. In this light, it was the color of rich honey. She looked younger without that severe knot at her nape. Younger and softer.

In those unguarded moments he saw her stretch her arms out, as if to embrace all of nature. On her face was a look of sheer joy. He felt almost reluctant to disturb her, knowing that the moment she became aware of him her guard would be back in place.

"One hour. As promised."

She turned. "Thank you. It was wonderful."

"You look refreshed." His gaze roamed appreciatively over her.

She flushed, wondering if he could tell that she wasn't wearing her underthings. She had washed them and spread them out discreetly behind a screen of foliage.

"Those things will never dry, you know." She followed his gaze, afraid for a moment that he was talking about her underwear. Instead, he indicated the heavy khaki pants and shirt.

"Yes, I'm aware that I've laid them out in a drizzle. But at least they're clean. And as soon as we've set up the tents I'll spread them out inside my tent, out of the rain."

He resisted the chance to follow through on that. "But even in a tent they won't dry, Ann. The air is too humid."

"Then I'll just have to put them back on damp," she said calmly. "At least they'll be clean."

"And the hiking boots?"

She glanced at them, hanging by their laces from the tree. "I suppose I'll just have to get used to wet feet."

"No." His curt response was tinged with irritation. Taking a breath, he tried to keep his tone reasonable. "Canvas shoes are really more practical, Ann. They allow your skin to breathe. In those hiking boots your feet will be continually wet, and in time you'll develop some real problems. It's called Jungle Rot. Those boots are useless. You'd save time and trouble to just leave them here and wear the canvas shoes."

"But Dr. Smythe-Fielding—"

"To hell with Dr. Smythe-Fielding!" He fought for a more patient tone. "I'm telling you those boots will give you real trouble. Stick to canvas sneakers."

She shot him a look of fury and held back the sharp response she wanted to hurl.

He watched her eyes narrow slightly. Swearing under his breath he decided to try a new tack.

"I'll bet you're hungry."

She swallowed her anger. "A little."

"Would you like to help me catch the fish, or would you rather decide on dessert?"

She laughed in spite of her momentary lapse into anger. "I've never fished before. I'd like to see how you do it."

"Never fished?" He studied her a moment. "I don't believe it. I thought everybody had gone fishing at least once in their life."

Shyly, she scuffed a bare foot in the grass. "No. Never went fishing. There are lots of things I've never done." She brightened. "But I'm willing to try. Will you teach me?"

He wanted to scoop her into his arms, hold her against him and promise to teach her everything in the world. Instead, he said quite casually, "Okay, Dr. Lowry. Let's go fishing."

Following him to the edge of the pool, she stopped. "I'll get soaked."

He thought a minute. "Roll those pants as high as you can. Then hope the water doesn't come up higher than that." He raised one eyebrow in a mock sinister expression. "Unless, of course, you'd like to just take off those things altogether."

"Why Dr. McFarland." She imitated his look, forcing one eyebrow up. "I do believe you have an evil mind."

He was so surprised at her sudden humor that he stared at her a moment before bursting into laughter.

"You're getting too smart for your britches. Come on. Just hold this end of the net, and when I tell you to drop it I expect you to drop it instantly." He brushed a lock of hair from her eyes. "Think you can handle this, doctor?"

"It is a most difficult assignment, but I'll do my best."

They spent over an hour standing in the pool while Jay drove fish toward the net and Ann dropped it at his command. When they had caught enough for a proper meal he led her back to shore.

"You did just fine, my dear doctor. I believe by tomorrow I may have you chasing the fish while I take on the very difficult task of dropping the net."

"I will, on one condition." She gave him a sly smile. "That you drop the net instantly. If I find that you can't take commands I'll have to look for another assistant."

He shook his head. "Give you a little responsibility and it goes right to your head. That may be the last time I take you fishing."

While Jay made a fire and set the fish sizzling in a skillet, Ann asked, "Is this all we're going to eat?"

He glanced around, then gave her a slow smile. "Are you kidding? Here in paradise there is more fruit than you can imagine. Which would you prefer? Papaya, bananas, pineapple?"

"Did you know," she interrupted, "that the pineapple is actually a member of the citrus family? It contains citric acid. That makes it a citrus."

He shook his head with a wry smile. "Did you know, Dr. Lowry, that you just sounded like a textbook again?"

She flushed. It was true. She couldn't seem to help

herself. These little bits of knowledge just poured out of her at the strangest times.

"I know," Jay said suddenly to ease her embarrassment. "How about taro? Have you ever heard of it?"

She nodded. "I'm a botanist, remember? Plants, especially exotic native plants, are my specialty. I know all about taro, but I've never tasted it."

"It's a staple here on the island. The tuberous roots are pounded or ground into a paste. I suppose you'd compare it to a mashed potato. Want to try it?"

She nodded. "Of course I do."

Together they searched the surrounding jungle, digging the tubers. Jay showed Ann how the natives used to pound them with primitive bones or rocks until they formed a starchy paste.

An hour later, Ann and Jay leaned their backs against a rock, enjoying a wonderful dinner.

Ann sighed. It had been a lovely first day in the rain forest. Jay had been good company, an excellent guide and except for an occasional bout of temper, unusually sensitive to her needs.

She smiled at him, her eyes warm in the firelight.

"It's growing dark. We'd better set up camp," he said, keeping his voice casual.

She shrugged. "All right. I think I'm ready for another chore."

He bent to his pack and removed a thick square of opaque material.

She walked up behind him. "Jay, where's my tent?"

He held up his hand. "This is our tent."

She blinked. "Our tent? What happened to mine?"

He forced his voice to remain as neutral as possible. "Your tent was heavy, Ann, and, frankly, outdated. Thanks to our space program, a much lighter, revolutionary material is used for tents now. It can be carried in a pocket and set up in a matter of minutes."

He glanced up, then, seeing her murderous expression, looked away and began assembling the tent. Over his shoulder he said, "It can easily accommodate both of us and all our supplies as well, so they will stay dry overnight. It's transparent, so that we can see out, in the event of stray animals coming too close during the night. And I think you'll be pleasantly surprised at the comfort."

Her voice was nearly strangled with fury. "I don't believe what I'm hearing. You can't possibly expect me to . . . sleep in the same tent with you."

With the simple assembly completed, he turned to face her. "Ann. We will be spending an entire month together. In that time, we will have walked over a hundred miles, crisscrossing every inch of this rain forest. You can't reasonably expect me to carry two separate tents and set them up every single night."

She faced him, hands on her hips, her mouth a thin line of anger. "Reasonable! You dare to talk about being reasonable! I never asked you to pitch my tent. I am very capable of setting up my own tent—every single night of the next month."

"Ah. But you did ask me to carry it, didn't you?"

"Oh!" She turned away, too furious to even argue. She could feel hot tears of anger sting her eyes. She whirled back. "I should have known better than to ask for your help. If only I had kept quiet and carried my own gear, none of this would have happened. How dare you presume to make my decisions for me! Jay McFarland, I have no intention of sleeping in the same tent with you!''

She stormed across the clearing, wishing there were some place she could go to escape him. In a state of terrible agitation she paced back and forth beside the pool, a million angry words rushing through her mind.

She hated him at this moment. Here she was, in the middle of an alien world, "his world," she realized bleakly, and she was at the mercy of a man who obviously intended to humiliate her.

She wouldn't let him. She couldn't. He had no right to force himself on her. If she had to stay out here all night to drive home her point, she would.

She paced furiously, considering how many ways to do away with the . . . bully inside that tent. She stopped, seeing the light of a lantern flick on. It bathed the tent and its occupant in an eerie green-gold light.

When he stepped outside the tent she whirled away, determined to prove to him that she wasn't in the least bit interested in what he was doing. She could hear him scurrying softly through the wet grass but she refused to turn around. She wouldn't give him the satisfaction of knowing that she was aware he was nearby.

In a matter of minutes the jungle sounds blotted out his footsteps and she stopped her pacing, wondering just what he was up to. She turned tentatively in the direction of the tent.

In the glow of the lantern she saw him standing inside

the tent, pulling his shirt over his head. Through the transparent fabric of the shelter she could see him quite clearly. He bent and draped his shirt over his backpack. Drawing back a blanket he lay down, then leaned over to turn off the lantern. Instantly the tent and its occupant were swallowed by darkness.

Ann's fists clenched at her sides. She gritted her teeth so tightly, her mouth ached. He hadn't given one thought to her safety. He was so unconcerned about her that he was simply ignoring her. She could be attacked by wild animals, drowned in that pool or lost in the dense jungle. Would Jay McFarland care? Absolutely not. He was going to sleep! While she seethed in impotent anger, that brute was calmly going to sleep.

Chapter Six

Ann huddled outside the tent for over an hour, until she hoped she had given Jay enough time to fall asleep. The fine mist was now a steady downpour, and though the temperature remained mild Ann was drenched to her skin.

Stealthily she made her way to the shelter. She paused just inside the tent, listening to the sound of steady, even breathing from the figure under the blanket. Satisfied that Jay was sleeping she began to move soundlessly across the open space. She paused at the sight of something spread out on a drying rack.

Her clothes. She was touched to realize that Jay had collected her wet clothing and draped it over a wooden rack for drying. That must have been what he was doing outside earlier.

That served to remind her to hurry back outside and retrieve her soaked underclothes. Wringing them out, she draped them alongside her other things, then felt inside her backpack for the nightgown she had packed. It was gone.

Gritting her teeth at her foolish mistake in allowing Jay to repack her belongings, she moved to his pack and began rummaging around. Her hand touched soft dry fabric, and she pulled the garment from the pack, running her fingertips along the cloth to determine what it was. From the size and shape she knew it had to be one of Jay's flowery shirts. Right now she didn't care how silly she might look in it. She had to get out of these wet clothes and into bed. She was soaked, chilled and ready to drop from exhaustion.

As quietly as possible she slipped out of her khaki pants and shirt and slipped on Jay's Hawaiian shirt. Having something dry next to her clammy skin felt wonderful. She quickly draped her soaked garments over the drying rack and, rubbing a towel roughly over her hair, slipped between the sheets.

Ann had expected to be sleeping on a cot or on an air mattress set on the ground. Neither would be soft nor luxurious. So she was shocked to feel a soft cushion of comfort beneath her. The bed, which stretched from one side of the tent to the other, felt as soft as down. Surprised, Ann tentatively felt around in the dark. Whatever this was made of, it was infinitely softer than any tent mattress she had ever slept on before.

Hoping to put as much distance between herself and

Jay as possible, Ann moved to the far edge of the tent and snuggled beneath the blankets.

"So you finally had enough sense to come in out of the rain."

She started at the deep voice. "I was hoping you were asleep by now." There was no mistaking the venom in her tone.

"How the hell could I be expected to sleep when I knew you were huddled out there in the pouring rain?"

She could hear him turn towards her in the darkness.

"Really? I didn't think you cared what happened to me." Ann hated her tone of voice. She realized she sounded like a pouting child, but she couldn't seem to help herself. She wanted him to know how upset she really was.

"Of course I care what happens to you."

She felt him prop himself up on one elbow in the blackness. She peered at him, but could see little except his form.

"Do you, Jay?" She felt a tiny flicker of warmth.

"Certainly. After all, I am your guide."

Her heart plummeted. "Yes, I suppose it would be difficult to explain to your father if I were to be somehow injured or lost while you were fast asleep in the comfort of your tent."

"Exactly." She thought she detected a smile in his voice, but she was too tired and angry to care.

After a prolonged silence he said, "Ann?"

She expelled an angry breath. "What now? I'm trying to sleep."

"What are you wearing in bed?"

"That's none of your business. Let me sleep, Jay."

There was a soft chuckle in the night. "I just thought it would give me something pleasant to dream about." After a long pause he whispered, "You did have enough sense to take off your wet clothes, I hope."

"Oh, for heaven's sake." She sat up in the darkness. "Will you please be quiet. You're not my keeper. I've been taking care of myself for many years. And I certainly have enough sense to take off soaked clothing before climbing into bed. Now go to sleep."

She lay back down and pulled the blanket over herself. He was closer now, and as he spoke his breath fanned her temple.

"When I sorted through your gear, I came across an ugly nightgown. It—"

"Ugly! How dare—"

"Yes. Ugly. It looked like something you might wear if you were fighting off a cold. It was some sort of shapeless, old-fashioned thing."

"Thank you very much. I rather liked that gown."

"I threw it out." She heard the laughter shaking his voice.

She gritted her teeth. "You had no right."

"That's true. But it's too late now."

She turned away.

"So?" She could feel him sitting up again, tugging at the blanket as he did. "Ann, answer me. What are you wearing?"

After a prolonged pause she said in an exasperated

voice, "Your shirt. Now, are you satisfied, Jay? Let me sleep."

"My shirt? You're really wearing my shirt? Let me see."

The light was snapped on, blinding her.

She sat up quickly, holding the blanket to her chin.

"Jay, if you don't turn off that light and let me—"

"Show me."

She glowered at him, then dropped the blanket just a fraction. It was enough to prove that she was indeed wearing his flowery shirt.

The red beard twitched as he smiled. His eyes danced with humor. "One small step for science, one giant step for man-woman relations."

She groaned and lay back down. The light was snapped off, enveloping them in blackness.

After an extended silence, she whispered, "Jay."

"What?"

She was startled that his voice sounded so near.

"This mattress is so soft. What's it made of?"

She heard the warmth of his chuckle. "Another wonder of the space age. It's a tightly woven fabric similar to that used in making parachutes. Between it is a layer of air bubbles. Deflated, it fits into a pocket. Inflated, it's as comfortable as a waterbed." He paused. "Have you ever slept on a waterbed?"

"No."

"It's wonderfully buoyant." There was a longer pause. Then, "They should be mandatory on honeymoons."

A hand brushed her hair, and Ann felt a tingle of warmth slide along her spine.

"Goodnight, little Annie Laurie. Sweet dreams."

An eerie light invaded the tent, bathing the sleeping figures in a hazy glow. The rain had once again gentled to a fine mist.

Ann awoke quickly, startled for a brief moment by the strange surroundings. Then she lay very still, enjoying a sense of déjà vu. Her most vivid memories as a child were of awaking in a tent alongside her parents, often in some remote and primitive site. She smiled, feeling a delicious warmth at the feelings such memories evoked.

Some children grew up surrounded by the aroma of cookies baking in a homey kitchen. Others would forever connect yellow school busses and bag lunches to their most familiar childhood memories. But for Ann, childhood meant journeys to countries with improbable names, in far-off places a continent away. Her parents had tutored her by lamplight, candlelight, even firelight. She wished they had instructed her on some of the basics of camping, too. But there had always been guides along to see to those necessities, and Ann, herself, had been too young to pay much attention.

She sighed, allowing herself a few precious moments of inactivity before hurling herself into the day. It had been so long since she had been in the field. The years of studying and then teaching at the university hadn't made her soft. She had continued to practice an inner discipline, as if unconsciously believing that one day she would get this opportunity.

She cast a furtive glance at the sleeping figure barely a foot away. He slept so peacefully. Assured that he was sound asleep, she allowed her gaze to linger on his handsome face. His lips, warm and firm, were parted in a smile, as if he were indulging in a pleasant dream. She had the strangest urge to run her fingertips over that beard, to assure herself that it was as soft as she remembered. There was strength and fierce pride in that face—and something more. Something she couldn't quite pinpoint. She would have said he possessed great strength of character. But somehow that didn't fit the impression she had of Jay McFarland. Though he professed to be dedicated to veterinary medicine, he appeared too casual. Ann always had the feeling that just below the surface there was teasing laughter, waiting to bubble forth. He was a puzzle to her. She had such conflicting emotions whenever she tried to figure him out.

She tore her gaze from him. This was her first full day in the field. There were so many experiments to conduct. So much to see and do. So little time.

She tossed back the blanket and bounded from the bed. Her lacy underclothes, draped over the wooden drying rack, had dried completely overnight. She was relieved to see that they would dry so quickly. Since they were all she had allowed herself to pack, they would have to do for the entire month. The khaki shirt and pants were still damp. Disappointed, she thrust her hand into the tall hiking boots. They were soaking wet.

"As long as you look that good in them, you may have all my clothes if you'd like."

She whirled at the sleepy, husky voice. "Turn around until I've dressed," she ordered.

"And deny myself the wonderful view from here? Not on your life."

"Jay." She adopted the tone she used with her students when all else failed. "I will not discuss this further. Turn around."

Chuckling, he slid beneath the blanket. Only his two hands could be seen, holding the covers over his head. His words were muffled. "Why not leave on my shirt, since it's dry, and just wear a pair of shorts?"

"Because I didn't pack any shorts. All I have are these khaki pants."

"That's no problem." The blanket dropped and Jay hurried to her side. "Give them to me, and I'll cut them down to shorts with my hunting knife."

Dressed only in a pair of cotton jogging shorts, he towered over her, exuding an overwhelming male virility.

She could feel the flush of embarrassment heat her throat and cheeks. She was practically naked in front of this man, and he was bounding around like a puppy, completely unaware of her predicament.

Of course he was practically naked as well. But she realized that wouldn't bother Jay in the least.

He pulled his knife from the pack and reached for the pants in her hand.

"Here. I'll just slice off the legs, and you'll have a nice, comfortable pair of shorts."

Ann eyed the pants for a long moment, undecided. "Won't I need the long pants to protect me from insect bites?"

He held up a small vial. "There's enough insect repellant in here to protect us both for months. It's completely odorless, colorless. I'm sure it won't harm even your delicate skin, Ann."

She was running out of arguments. Besides, the thought of comfortable shorts was tempting. Yesterday, on the long trek through the rain forest, the heavy khaki fabric had clung to her skin like a weight.

"I suppose it wouldn't hurt to cut off one pair of pants. I'll still have a second pair if I decide I don't like it." She handed the pants to Jay, forcing herself not to stare at his burly chest. "All right, go ahead and cut these off." She held her thumb and finger where she wanted him to make the cut, just above the knee.

Jay took them from her hand and turned slightly, slicing quickly through the fabric. With a ripping sound, he tore the rest of the fabric. Except for a few dangling threads, they tore neatly.

While he was busy with her pants, Ann hurriedly scooped up her dry underthings and primly tucked them into her pack. It just wasn't proper to leave them out where they would be seen. Besides, she remembered how Jay had teased her about her frilly feminine apparel back at the house.

As Jay handed back the pants Ann realized that he had cut them much shorter than she had indicated. They would be scandalously brief. With a quick glance at the bland expression on his face, she assured herself that it had been an innocent mistake.

He turned away before she could detect the light that danced in his dark eyes. "As long as my shirt is already on you, and dry, you may as well wear it today and hope your khaki shirt dries by tomorrow." As she began to protest, he added quickly, "It's no problem. I have a spare shirt."

"All right. Thank you. Now, if you'll just turn your back to me for a minute, I'll finish dressing."

Ann fumbled with the shorts, her fingers awkward because she was hurrying. Jay's shirt hung nearly to her knees, and the short sleeves billowed to her elbows. Even after the shorts were buttoned, the excess material of the shirt hung out of the waistband, down around her hips.

Jay turned and, realizing her dilemma, began to roll the sleeves until they were at the top of her arms. She felt the beginnings of a tingling sensation at his intimate touch.

Then he caught the tails of the shirt. "Here. Just tie this thing up like this." He tied the shirt just beneath her midriff, knotting the fabric at the end to keep it in place. As he tied, his knuckles brushed the softness of her breasts.

She flinched, and confusion clouded her eyes. Glancing up at his face, she saw the laughter crinkling his eyes, twitching his beard. Gratefully, she realized he was going to let the incident pass without comment. She would have fled the tent if he had begun teasing her.

"What is this scar?" His finger traced a thin line

which began at her midriff and circled nearly to her back.

"It's an old scar. From . . . an accident."

"It looks like a pretty bad cut. Auto accident?"

He realized that she had gone very still, and he cursed himself for causing her discomfort.

"No. An . . . airplane accident when I was twelve. My parents were killed. I survived."

"I'm sorry." He studied her profile as she turned her face away from his scrutiny. "Where were you flying to?"

"We were flying in a small plane across eastern Africa. It was on the first leg of our return home. My parents and I had been living in Kenya for over a year."

He remembered her tension when she'd walked off the small interisland plane on the day she arrived. How had she found the courage to fly in a small craft after living through such a tragedy?

"No brothers or sisters?" He knotted a fist at his side. Why was he pursuing this now? She was such a private person that he was amazed she forced herself to respond.

"No. My father had a brother, my uncle Frank. He took me home to live with him."

"You were lucky to have someone."

"Yes."

Her tone, he noted, was without emotion.

He lifted her chin, forcing her to meet his gaze. "I like your hair like this." His fingers trailed the tawny waves that bounced above her shoulders.

She swallowed, uncomfortable with the compliment, but relieved that he had deftly changed the subject.

"Thank you. I'm afraid I won't be able to pin it up for the rest of the month. I seem to have lost the pins when I went swimming yesterday. I know I set them on a small flat rock. But when I looked for them they were gone." She glanced up to meet his steady gaze. "I might be willing to accuse a certain guide of taking them, except that you were in the forest while I was washing my hair and swimming. Besides, what would you possibly want with my hairpins?"

"Well, I'm sure the birds around here won't mind if you don't pin your hair back. And your friendly guide isn't complaining." He smiled blandly. "Now, why don't I start a fire and make some coffee?"

"Good idea. I'll make up two bowls of my high-protein food supplement."

"Ugh." As Jay walked away his fingers tightened around the cluster of hairpins in his pocket. He would have to remember to bury them under a rock when he was alone. A twinkle of laughter lit his blue eyes.

Within an hour they had finished their breakfast and packed their gear.

Jay glanced at the heavy military boots laced incongruously up Ann's bare ankles.

"You really should wear canvas shoes, Ann. They're much lighter for walking, and they'll be healthier for your feet."

"I'll stick with the hiking boots. Dr. Smythe-Fielding said you never know what you might step on in a rain forest."

He shrugged. He had won enough battles for one day. There was always tomorrow.

With a lingering backward glance at the lovely pool and waterfall, Ann followed Jay deep into the forest.

The morning was gone before they found a site that Ann wanted to study. While Jay set up their camp, Ann eagerly began the preliminary work. Soil samples were taken and carefully labeled. With her photographic equipment set up she took pictures of the site. With special lenses even the smallest plants could be photographed in minute detail.

Long after Jay had set up their tent and hunted nearby for food for their lunch and dinner, Ann was still working diligently on her project. Fascinated by her nervous energy, Jay found a dry spot beneath a tree and, leaning his back against the rough bark, lit a cigar and watched in silence for a long time. Finally he broke through her concentration.

"Dad said your work will leave its mark in the scientific community."

She sat back on her heels and clicked off several more photos before replying.

"Maybe. The opportunity to study the flora of this unique island will make a tremendous difference to my work. That's why I can't waste a precious day. There's so little time in a month."

He heard a quivering impatience in her voice, and he felt a surge of emotion that startled him.

For the rest of the day, until the light faded, he was content to leave her alone to concentrate on her work.

*   *   *

Just after dinner a heavy downpour drove them to the shelter of their tent. Ann sat crosslegged beside the battery-operated lantern, writing in her journal. Round glasses perched on her nose, giving her an owlish look.

Jay sat on the opposite side of the tent, smoking, trying to read a colleague's paper which he had brought along. It was impossible to concentrate. He found his gaze drawn to the small figure bathed in light, bent over the book in her lap. He remembered the prim young woman in his father's study, and mentally compared her to the woman he now watched.

Silken blond waves cascaded around her face and shoulders. Every so often she unconsciously tucked a strand of hair behind her ear. Within a few minutes it would drift loose and brush her cheek.

He stared at the shadowed cleft in the deep neckline of her flowery shirt. He could make out the soft swell of her breasts. Something fluttered in the pit of his stomach. He found himself wondering what this little creature had done to bewitch him like this.

The pale skin exposed at her bared midriff was firm above a flat stomach. He mentally measured the width of her slim hips.

She had taken off the hiking boots and stuffed them with wadded paper in the hope of absorbing some of the moisture. He studied her toes—such soft, pink toes. They shouldn't be jammed into those military boots. If she didn't soon give in to his suggestion to switch to canvas shoes, he'd take matters into his own hands.

His hand clenched and unclenched. She hadn't made another remark about the tent. He realized she was trying to make the best of a bad bargain. A smile twitched about his lips. It violated every one of her principles, he knew, to have to share this tent with him. But he'd been forced into this decision when he saw her outdated tent and realized just how determined she was to have her own way.

She glanced up at that moment and caught the dark frown of concentration on his face.

"I'm sorry, Jay. Am I keeping you up with this light?"

"No. Of course not. I have a lot of reading to catch up on." He held up the paper as if to prove his statement.

"The light is better here." She stood, and he tried not to be too obvious as he studied her shapely legs. "I'm going to turn in now anyway, so you may as well use this lantern for your reading."

Before he could protest she handed him the lantern and fished in her pack for something dry. At long last, the khaki shirt had dried enough for her to wear it as a nightshirt. She could now lay out the flowery shirt and shorts for the morning. If they proved to be too damp, she would wear the others.

"If you don't mind turning around for a few minutes, I'd like to slip out of these wet things."

Jamming the cigar into his mouth he turned to the side of the tent. He wanted to tell her a few things about this foolishness, but hearing her haughty tone he decided it was still too soon. But before long . . .

"All right." Her tone was even. "Thank you, Jay. And goodnight."

He glowered at her back as she pulled the blanket up to her chin.

Her voice drifted over her shoulder. "You can leave the light on as long as you please. I'm so tired, nothing could keep me awake. Goodnight."

"'Night."

Jay sat with the paper in his lap, the reading light glaring in the corner of the tent. For long minutes he stared at the quiet form in the bed.

When he was certain she was asleep he moved across the tent. Taking his knife from his pack, he held up Ann's khaki pants and spare shirt. She was the most obstinate woman he'd ever met. These clothes were far too heavy for this tropical climate. But she would never admit her mistake. The only solution was to take matters into his own hands, as usual.

At last, with a sigh of resignation, he removed his clothes, slipped into a pair of dry jogging shorts and crawled into bed. The figure beside him didn't move. But he was aware of her with every fiber of his being. Aware of her haunting perfume, which reminded him of the tiny Passion Flower here in the jungle. Aware of the silken cloud of hair that begged for his touch. Aware of her thigh just inches from his. Aware of every breath she took.

Chapter Seven

It was barely dawn. The pale amber light of the rain forest had not yet penetrated the tent. Ann stretched, then lay back a moment, allowing herself these few magic moments of complete relaxation before starting another day of work.

With one hand she smoothed the heavy shirt in which she had slept. Her sheer bikini briefs felt cool against her skin.

She was aware of a sudden tension in the figure beside her. Jay was awake, instantly alert.

"How did you sleep?"

She realized she loved the husky quality of his voice in the morning.

"Like a rock. I don't think I moved the whole night." She laughed. "Nothing like a day of good hard work to knock you out for the night."

"Um. I can think of nicer ways to fall asleep."

She stiffened, feeling a sudden tenseness in every part of her body. Why did he have to tease her this way, constantly putting her on notice that he was ready to pounce? Now she would have to put up her guard. Now she would have to remind herself once again to be aware of him as a man.

She tossed aside the blanket and hurried to her clothes. She might as well get dressed and start her work.

With a little gasp she stopped, then held up her khaki pants and shirt.

"What in the world . . . ?"

Jay watched with the barest hint of a smile curling his lips.

She turned on him with blazing eyes. "You cut off my pant legs and shirt sleeves. Why?"

He looked offended. "Me? How can you accuse me of such a thing?"

"There are only two of us in this rain forest, Jay. You and I. And I know I didn't get up in the middle of the night and cut my own clothes."

"Then it must have been the *menehunes.*"

"*Menehunes!*" She dropped her hands to her sides, still clutching her clothes, and glared at him. "What are they?"

"The little people of the forest. The natives say they're strong, ambitious, gentle people, who only come out at night. By dawn they complete their project and disappear into the mist of the forest." He folded his hands beneath his head and gave her a smug smile.

"You're very lucky the *menehunes* liked you well enough to do this for you. They only take on special projects, you know."

"Um-hmm." She was standing, hands on hips, surveying him with a cool look. "Lucky little me." With a vicious toss she threw her handful of clothes at him, hitting him in the head.

Surprised, he grabbed the pants and hurled them back. With one hand she caught them. Before she could throw them again he surged up from the bed and caught her in a tackle, bringing her down on the bed with him on top of her.

Jay was wearing nothing but his cotton jogging shorts. His chest was bare. She could feel the tickle of the dark hair of his legs against her legs.

She managed to get one hand free and tugged hard on his shaggy head before he pinned her hand beneath her. Catching her other hand, he locked it behind her, then laughed as she tried to pull free.

Her breath was coming in short little gasps from the effort. "Little people. Hah! One member of their group is over six feet tall. I don't call that little."

"All right. Time to confess. I was the villain. It was I who cut off your pant legs and shirt sleeves. Not the *menehunes*. But if I hadn't done it, they would have."

Her eyes narrowed. She tried to turn her head. "But you had no right."

"I had to take charge of the situation. You were never going to admit that those clothes were all wrong for this climate. I've watched you swelter in that get-up. I've seen how heavy those things get when they're wet. It's like carrying around extra pounds. But still you refused to admit you made a mistake. So now, Miss Prim and Proper, there's no room left to argue. It's done.''

"Oh, Jay McFarland, I'd like to . . .''

"Thank me? By all means, Dr. Lowry. Be my guest.''

She glared at the silly grin on his face.

"Let me go, Jay.''

"Not yet.''

"Then at least let my hands loose.''

"So you can slap my face? I'm not that stupid.'' He grinned, his face hovering just inches above hers. His body was pressed tightly to hers.

Her breasts were flattened beneath his weight. His hips pressed hers into the softness of the mattress.

It had started as a silly fight and Ann was still angry at his heavy-handed tactics. But she was becoming aware of the subtle change in the pressure of his hands, which still held hers tightly. At the change of his touch, her slender body seemed to strain toward his. Ever so slowly, the look on his face softened. His touch gentled. His face descended to hers until his lips were almost brushing her mouth.

He whispered, "You're welcome.''

Somewhere inside her a nerve tightened. Her voice was barely a strangled whisper. "I didn't thank you.''

"Oh, but you're about to.'' His lips moved gently over hers, teasing, coaxing.

"Jay, please . . .''

Her eyes, he noticed, had grown even larger. A glorious sunrise filtered its rays through the tent, sending shafts of liquid honey across the bed. In the muted light she looked like a golden girl—the wild tangle of hair, the pale ivory skin, the wide amber eyes—all taking on the sun's glow.

"Annie, Annie." Her name was a caress on his lips as he brought his mouth to hers.

The kiss was so exquisitely tender, she became lost in it. Her heart told her there was nothing to fear from this gentle giant. He held her as if she were a fragile doll. His fingers twined in the tangles of her hair, drawing her head upward toward him.

Wrapped in his arms, feeling his body imprinting itself on hers as he pressed her to the mattress, Ann became lost in the overpowering wonder of this man who held her. His shaggy beard was soft against her face. His faintly musky, masculine scent stirred her senses. His hair-roughened chest and legs excited her.

He rolled onto his side to ease the weight of his body from hers, and drew her with him. There was strength in his embrace, tempered by a fierce tenderness. He folded her closer and kissed her temples, her eyelids, the tip of her nose.

His hand slipped beneath her shirt and he felt her startled reaction. Ever so gently he ran his fingertips along her back until he felt her gradually relax under his soothing touch. Then his lips found hers, and she forgot everything except the pleasure his lips and hands were giving.

His tongue traced the outline of her lips until, groaning, she opened her mouth to accept him. The kiss became more possessive, more demanding.

Her arms lifted, taking him into her embrace. Her hands roamed his shaggy hair, drawing his head down to hers. She kissed him hungrily, wanting more.

When he lifted his head her fingertips traced the growth of his beard, then followed the outline of his lips. He laughed in delight at her sudden boldness and, rolling onto his back, caught her in his arms and pulled her on top of him.

Once more she was startled, and he could feel her sudden resistance to his touch. Her body was pressed to his, her legs straddling his. With feather-soft caresses his fingertips roamed her back until, with almost no will of her own, her hands reached out to his face.

He gave her a gentle smile. "Bonnie little Annie. Give me your kiss."

She lowered her lips until they touched his. She heard his sudden intake of breath before his arms came around her in a fierce embrace. His hands were everywhere, molding her to his length, pressing her hips to his, finding the soft swell of breast beneath the khaki shirt.

She had never let a man kiss her like this before, touch her like this before. And yet it was the sweetest ecstacy she had ever known. She felt she was drowning in waves of passion.

The tempo of their lovemaking changed suddenly. The simmering passion, so long held at bay, strained for release. The hands that had gently caressed now stoked a raging fire. The lips that had tempted and coaxed were now demanding.

He rolled once more to his side, taking her with him.

His strong arms held her to him, making her achingly aware of his arousal.

Jay's lips found the hollow of her throat, sending impulses sparking along her spine. As his lips moved lower, his fingers fumbled with the buttons of her shirt until that barrier fell away, exposing her ivory skin to his touch.

She had never known such exquisite pleasure, as his lips moved from one breast to the other and her nipples tautened at his touch. Deep inside her, strange new sensations were born. His practiced seduction was taking her to the edge of reason.

"Jay. Please stop." She touched her fingers to his lips, then raised wide, luminous eyes to his. "Help me, Jay. I've never . . . please."

The kiss died. His hands stilled. He rolled away from her, leaving her feeling hollow, empty. She could hear him taking deep breaths to steady himself. The mattress sagged beneath his weight as he fought to keep from reaching out to her.

For long moments the only sound in the tent was labored breathing, punctuated by an occasional sigh.

Finally Ann sat up, holding her shirt together with one hand. The other hand reached up to comb trembling fingers through a tawny, tangled cloud.

Jay sat up at the edge of the mattress. She studied his broad shoulders, his bowed head. Tentatively she reached out a hand to touch his shoulder.

"Don't." His voice was strangled. She heard him take a deep breath. "Don't touch me yet, Ann."

Shocked, she realized just how far they had gone. Even now Jay was fighting off an almost overwhelming desire to continue this to its natural conclusion.

Her voice was soft, breathless. "I'm sorry, Jay. This should never have happened. I never meant it to go so far."

"I did." He cocked his head to one side and regarded her shocked expression.

After long minutes of silence he stood. "There's a pool not far from here. I'm going swimming for about an hour." The laugh he attempted became a ragged sound. "I need the exercise."

He turned to study her, still huddled in the middle of the mattress. She looked so small and vulnerable, legs tucked under her. She was still grasping the shirt with shaking fingers, trying to maintain some dignity. Her hair spilled in wild disarray about her face. Even now her lips looked soft, inviting. There was no help for it. He wanted her. If he could have, he would have taken her now.

He swore under his breath and whirled away impatiently.

Ann glanced up at the fading light, and decided to call it a day. She worked quickly, efficiently, tagging the plants, snapping off the last pictures, jotting notes.

Her mouth watered at the wonderful aroma of something cooking. Jay constantly surprised her with the variety of their menu.

In the days since their torrid scene in the tent they had

maintained a respectful distance. Ann realized with a grim smile that the quality of her work had improved markedly since then. With nothing to focus her nervous energy on except her experiments, she had thrown herself into a frenzy of work.

At night she wrote in her journal until exhaustion drove her to bed. During the daylight hours she worked such long hours that Jay sometimes had to remind her to stop and eat.

Both of them were operating on the fine edge of their nerves. And both of them seemed to be poised on the brink, waiting for the next explosion.

She closed her notebook, jammed it into her pack and slowly walked to the tent set up in a small clearing.

Ann avoided Jay's pointed stare. It was something she did routinely now. He scowled. She hid. She frowned. He took long walks.

With a sigh she removed her wet hiking boots and winced in sudden pain. Surprised, she pulled off soaked socks and examined the swollen, reddish soles of her feet. White-hot pain seared the flesh, causing her to catch her breath at its intensity.

She sat for long moments, pondering her dilemma. If she told Jay about the pain he might know how to relieve it. For a field trip of this length he was a walking pharmacy. But given his brooding moods lately, he would be certain to remind her for the next weeks how foolish she had been not to take his advice and wear canvas shoes. She wondered if bearing the pain in her feet might not be easier than bearing Jay's smug attitude.

In a fit of anger she tossed a boot clear across the tent. Why did that man always have to be right?

Grabbing up her toiletries' case and a towel, she emerged from the tent in bare feet.

"Dinner is ready." Jay lifted a sizzling skillet from the fire.

"I'll be back in a few minutes." Ann swung the towel over her shoulder, forcing herself to walk normally despite the pain. "I want to grab a bath in the pool."

Puzzled, he watched her walk away, then turned his attention to the steaming coffee in his mug.

Ann removed her clothes and slid into the refreshing waters of the crystal pool. The rain forest was dotted with these rock basins, catching the runoff from the mountain cliffs above. The water sparkled like amber wine, colored, like everything else, by the filtered rays of the sun.

For a few moments the cool water was a shock against the hot pain in her feet. Then, as she eased herself deeper into the pool, she grew accustomed to the water and relaxed, enjoying the soothing coolness against her heated flesh.

She shampooed her hair, watching the foam drift toward the edge of the pool. Afterward, she lathered her body and ducked beneath the water, feeling deliciously refreshed.

Reluctantly she pulled herself from the pool and toweled herself dry, then slipped into the spare pair of khaki cut-offs and shirt. The pants had been chopped so short, they were practically indecent. The shirt now fell only to her ribs, and she tied the ends at her midriff. The sleeves had been cut off at the shoulder line.

For a moment she stared at the clothes Jay had fashioned with his hunting knife, and a tiny smile played about her lips. He had been right, of course. The fabric really was all wrong for this climate. But she never would have admitted her error.

That man, she mused, was like a bulldozer, going through life knocking down any obstacle that stood in his way. His way. She frowned. Everything had to be his way. He was so arrogant, so smug, so certain that he was always right.

She paused at the edge of the clearing. He had stripped off his shirt and stood squarely, with legs apart. His hands were raised, holding an ax. As he brought it down to split a log she watched the ripple of muscle along his back and shoulders. The motion was as smooth as a gymnast going through a routine. He stood the log on end, raised the ax a second time and cleanly split the log in an effortless rhythm.

His body was lean and hard, an athlete's body. Wide, muscled shoulders tapered to slim waist and hips. His legs were sturdy, well muscled from a lifetime of walking. His skin was bronzed, making a lovely contrast to his red-brown hair.

As he dropped another log on the fire, Ann forced herself to walk normally back to the tent, where she returned her toiletries and towel. Barefoot, she sat crosslegged near the fire and breathed in the lovely aroma of the dinner he had prepared.

"Something smells wonderful."

"Good. I'm glad you're hungry for a change." He set sizzling fish on a plate, along with taro.

They ate in companionable silence, relaxed, enjoying the sudden flashes of color as brilliantly hued birds darted from tree to tree. It was a neverending kaleidoscope of color in the forest.

Jay sensed something different about her. He couldn't quite put his finger on it. Over the past few days he had become even more aware of her, sensitive to every little nuance of her personality. This evening there seemed a brittle cheerfulness about her that wasn't quite natural. It seemed forced. She was hiding something. And he was determined to discover what it was. Living so intimately with her, he had no doubt that he would figure it out before long.

While Jay banked the fire, Ann slipped into the tent to change into dry clothes for the night and to record in her daily journal. When he entered the tent a short time later, she was bent over the pages, writing furiously.

He admired her discipline. There had been nights when he sensed that she was so weary she wanted to drop. But she faithfully recorded all her experiments in a daily log.

At last she closed the notebook and glanced up.

"Would you like the lantern?"

He nodded his head. "Yes. No rush, though. I'll be there in a minute."

She placed her journal and pen in the backpack and stood. The searing pain jolted her, and for the briefest moment she winced. Carefully composing her features, she forced herself to walk slowly to the far side of the tent, where she could gratefully lie down. She bit her lip at the effort it cost her and sank to the bed. She had done it. Hopefully, by morning her feet would be improved.

"Ann."

Poised to slip beneath the covers, she glanced up at his sharp tone. "Yes?"

Jay's eyes watched her closely. "Something's wrong."

"Yes. I'm very tired. Goodnight." She lifted the blanket and lay down quickly.

In long strides he was across the space that divided them. For a moment he towered over her, hands on hips. She clutched the blanket to her chin and turned her face away from that dark look.

"Let me see your feet."

"Don't be ridiculous!" She drew the blanket even higher, covering her nose and mouth.

He knelt and pulled away the covers. Ann was so afraid of his reaction to her feet that she forgot about her extreme modesty. His flowery shirt, which had become her usual nightshirt, rode up over her hips. Her only other item of clothing was her pair of sheer bikini briefs.

She could have been clad in armor. Jay was so intent on the condition of her feet he didn't even seem to see her.

"My God!" As he lifted first one foot and then the other, his face darkened in fury. "How could I have been so careless?"

"Dr. Smythe-Fielding . . ."

"Ah yes, the good Dr. Smythe-Fielding. Tell me. Just when did he explore our rain forest?"

She shrugged. "When he and your father were young. I think he said the late thirties or early forties."

Through gritted teeth he snarled, "In other words, forty or fifty years ago, the good doctor tramped through our rain forest, and that makes him an expert." He glowered at her so fiercely, she flinched. "I don't ever want to hear that name again. Not ever, do you hear?"

She bit her lip and fell silent.

He ran a finger critically over the sole of her foot, careful not to cause her any more pain than was necessary. Swearing under his breath, he gently set down her foot and lifted the other. "I knew this could happen, and I ignored it."

At first Ann looked away, unable to face him. Now, hearing him berate himself, she studied his face, which was set in tight, angry lines.

"This certainly isn't your fault, Jay. You tried to warn me about the boots." Her voice took on a softer tone. "It doesn't hurt too much. By morning.. . ."

"In the morning, we're leaving."

"What!" She stared at him, her face going ashen in the lamplight. "I'm not leaving. There's still so much ground to cover. Why I've—"

"I said we're leaving at first light. I warned you in the beginning, Ann. I'm not only your guide, I'm in charge here. What I say goes. And I say we're going home tomorrow."

From his pack he removed a tube of ointment. Tenderly he applied it to both her feet, then wrapped them in gauze. Without a word he drew the blanket over her, returned the ointment to his pack and snapped off the light.

Numbly, Ann watched his shadowy figure move about the tent as he removed his shirt and shoes before crawling into bed.

Go back! She couldn't go back. She had spent too much time and effort in preparation for this month in the rain forest. All the years of study. All the books, the papers, the theses she had written and read.

"Jay." Her voice pleaded in the darkness. "Please. I can't go back. Don't you understand what this means to me?"

His back was to her. His voice sounded weary. "I don't think you understand how serious this can be if we don't control it right at the beginning. I won't see you suffer, Ann. My mind is made up."

She sat up, tugging the blanket slightly as she did. "I'll suffer much more if I can't complete my work here. I'll never have this opportunity again. Please, Jay. I'm begging you. Don't make me leave."

He snapped on the light and faced her. She stared at him, imploring.

"It was my false pride that caused this, Jay." Her voice lowered in humiliation. "You've been right about everything. My tent. My clothes. I couldn't stand to admit that you were right about the boots too. The more you badgered me to wear the canvas shoes, the more

. . . obstinate I became." She spread her hands, beseeching him to understand. "Please don't send me away from here. Please."

For long moments he studied her, huddled against the side of the tent, looking lost in his big shirt. "Damn it! Don't you ever cry?"

At his unexpected outburst, her eyes widened a fraction before she looked down. Her head shook slightly. "No." It was barely more than a whisper. "My uncle wouldn't permit it. He said crying never solved anything. And he was right. He said if I cried he would send me away."

Jay's lips thinned to a tight, angry line. What kind of fool had that uncle been! Didn't he understand what he had done to a lonely, frightened child?

Her hair drifted about her cheeks and shoulders like a silken veil, shielding her face from him. He reached over and lifted it, allowing the strands to sift through his fingers. He wanted to take her in his arms and rock her like a child. Like the child she was never allowed to be.

His voice gentled. "Go to sleep now, Ann. The decision is mine, and you'll just have to accept it."

He snapped off the light, leaving them in darkness. He could feel her slip beneath the covers and turn her back to him. He strained against the darkness, but he heard no sound of weeping. Only the sky wept. The woman beside him kept her silent council.

He reached out a hand in the dark and brushed her cheek. She stiffened at his touch and sat up, huddled once more into the corner of the tent.

"Ann." He forced himself to keep his voice as soft as the velvet night. "Your uncle was wrong. It's perfectly all right to cry. Sometimes, in fact, it helps. It's a release. We all need to release our feelings sometimes."

He moved closer and reached out a hand to her shoulder. She flinched. He stroked her arm and shoulder gently, then moved closer, bringing his other hand up to touch her head.

She was trembling. He could feel the tremors wracking her frail body.

"Annie. Little Annie," he crooned, wrapping her in his embrace. "I wouldn't hurt you for anything in this world. Believe that."

"Oh Jay." The sigh seemed torn from her heart. "You just don't understand. This means more to me than anything. You can't send me away."

He heard the break in her voice, and realized how close she was to losing control.

"Annie," he whispered against her temple. "I want to do what's best for you. I'll reserve judgment until tomorrow. But if I send you away it won't be because you cried."

He felt the shuddering begin and then, finally, the tears of a lifetime were released. She cried as if her heart had broken. And all the while Jay held her as tenderly as if she were a fragile child. There was no passion in his touch. He wouldn't allow it. Right now, what Ann needed was a different kind of love. He was shocked at the depth of his feelings for her. Now she could cry as a child, and he could hold her as tenderly as any father.

But the love he felt surging through him was that of a man for a woman. A wonderful, obstinate, slowly emerging woman.

All through the night he held her, allowing the tears to flow freely until, drained, she slept in his embrace. Whatever passion he felt was carefully held at bay. Tonight he had the strength to be whatever she needed. And she needed the security to be herself—without any teasing, without any criticism.

Chapter Eight

Slender fingers of pink and gold streaked the sky high above the lush rain forest. Filtering through the canopy of jungle growth, a hazy shower of golden rays cast their benediction over the figures in the tent.

Ann stirred and found herself pinned beneath a warm weight. Her lashes fluttered. Her eyelids felt grainy from crying. Opening her eyes, she realized she was being held against Jay's length; one of his strong arms was flung across her, pinning her firmly to him.

For long moments she lay very still, unwilling to disturb his sleep. Memories of the previous night's highly emotional scene flooded her mind. She closed her eyes, nearly groaning aloud in humiliation. How could she have cried in front of him? How could she have allowed herself to expose such raw emotions in his presence?

What would he think of her now? She had managed to shatter the myth that she was a scientist, a dedicated professional. He wouldn't even be able to see her as an adult, a woman. He would remember only the silly, childish image of an overly emotional . . . crybaby.

She cringed at the thought of that word. Her uncle had hurled that epithet at her when she had first arrived at his forbidding university apartment. Alone, afraid, newly arrived from an extended hospital confinement, a bewildered Ann had numbly realized that her parents were really gone forever, and that this sterile place and this stranger would be home and family. He had led her to a cot in the library, explaining that it would be her room until he could make other arrangements. When he returned that evening from the university he found her huddled on the bed, crying out her grief. Unable to cope with a child's tears, this carefully bred gentleman had impulsively ordered her to stop, or he would send her away. He would never know what terror he had planted in her innocent heart.

Ann trembled, and the figure beside her stirred. As he turned his head, the soft beard tickled her cheek. Despite raw emotions that lay very close to the surface, she found herself smiling at that touch.

"Good morning." His gaze roamed over her features, as if to assure himself that she was all right.

She turned to meet his gaze. "Good morning, Jay. I'm . . . sorry about that scene last night."

"I'm not." His arm moved stiffly as he removed it from around her, and he stretched before sitting up. "How do you feel, Ann?"

"I feel fine. Terrific."

"Let's take a look at your feet." He knelt over her.

"Before you do, Jay, please listen to me." She rushed on, afraid he would interrupt. "The pain is gone. I feel wonderful, really I do. And I want you to know that I can continue my field research, without any problems. I'm not going to faint or get all feverish and cause you any problems. I may be small, but I'm very healthy and quite strong. I had a complete physical before I left home. The doctor assured—"

He placed a hand over her mouth.

Her eyes grew wide as he grinned.

"The next thing I know you'll be offering to show me your teeth, to prove what good stock you come from." He chuckled. "Ann, I'm sure you're not consumptive, weak-minded or morally depraved. But at the moment all I'm interested in is your feet."

She simmered at his attempt at humor. The friendly, almost pleading tone was gone. "I have to be allowed to continue my work."

"I'll be the judge of that." He pulled back the blanket and lifted one foot. Quickly unwrapping the gauze, he examined the foot, then lifted the second and did the same.

Her heart felt stuck somewhere in her throat.

"Well?"

He raised one eyebrow and studied her face.

"They're somewhat improved this morning."

She couldn't swallow. Couldn't blink. The look she gave him was so imploring, he finally allowed a half-smile.

"Does that mean I can stay here and go on with my work?"

"It means that your feet are probably just inflamed from being confined in those boots for so long. If so, a couple of days could make all the difference."

He reached for the ointment and gently applied a fresh coating and new gauze. While he worked he explained, "We're presently on the far northern side of the rain forest. Not far from here, only a few miles in fact, is the extreme northern edge of our island. The climate is very hot and dry, much like the American Southwest. Almost desert, with little rainfall and a long stretch of white sand." He glanced up at her questioning look. "I'll give you an option. Instead of calling off the trip, we could take a few days in the desert. A drying-off period, if you like. And if I see a marked improvement in your feet we'll come back and complete the month."

The relief she felt was apparent in her expressive features. She could have kissed him.

"Oh yes, Jay. Could we try it?"

He nodded. "You're not to walk. I'll break camp and leave everything here. After I carry you out, I'll come back for our gear."

She was appalled. "Carry me! I won't allow it. I can certainly walk a few miles."

He stood up, towering over her. "You have absolutely no vote in this. I told you, I'm in charge. Now, I can carry you to the northern shore of the island, or I can carry you back to the jeep."

She bit back an angry response and rolled to her side, refusing to look at him.

For long moments he stared down at her. Then he walked outside the tent and began the morning ritual of preparing breakfast before breaking camp. All the while he worked, he whistled cheerfully. Inside the tent, Ann listened in silence, aware that although she would have to submit to being carried, she had won a reprieve. And if her feet continued to respond to his tender ministrations, she would achieve a victory. Another chance to complete her field research. Her heart thudded against her ribs as she admitted something she had been denying. It was much more than the possibility of continuing the field trip that caused her pulse to race. It was the chance to spend a few more weeks alone with Jay.

Ann stretched out on the white sandy beach and sighed with pleasure.

The trip had been surprisingly easy. Despite her reluctance at being carried, Jay had made the task appear simple. With ease, he'd scooped her into his strong arms and begun tramping through the dense undergrowth. He stopped frequently to allow her to rest on boulders or to lie for a few minutes beneath the shelter of a tree. Throughout it all, a gentle mist fell on her upturned face, frizzing her hair, matting her eyelashes.

Jay's shaggy hair was also frizzed from the mist. With one arm about his neck, she allowed herself the luxury of touching the hair that curled above the collar of his damp shirt. It was intoxicating to be so near, inhaling his wonderful musky scent. Held close to his heart, she listened to the strong, steady beat, feeling oddly comforted by the sound.

He settled her on the sand, near the shelter of an

outcropping of rocks, before returning to the clearing in the forest for their gear.

He had exacted a promise from her that she would only walk when it was absolutely necessary. She agreed to stay off her feet as much as possible for the next few days.

Her gaze wandered over this strange, almost primitive setting. In the distance, high cliffs dropped into the sea. From here she could see the veil of mist that marked the entrance to the rain forest. Beyond lay lush vegetation.

Here on shore the scene was one of rock, white sand and relentless sunshine. There was little vegetation. There was also no sign of civilization. This inhospitable environment did not encourage development. The natives chose instead to live on the southern side of the island, where the climate was more tropical.

The McFarland island was a land of wide contrasts. Ann was only beginning to see just how fascinating it would be to live here, far from the bustling life in the city.

By early afternoon Jay had set up their tent, changed the dressings on Ann's feet and set off with a fishing pole across his shoulder in search of their dinner.

When he returned he had something more than dinner.

"What's this?" Ann asked as he dropped a piece of brightly colored fabric in her lap.

"I found the remains of a camp about a mile up the shoreline," he explained. "Someone had left this to dry in a palm tree."

"What am I supposed to do with it?"

He grinned impishly. "Wear it."

"This little thing?" She held it up, mentally measuring how much of herself would be covered.

"Yes. You wrap it about you, like a sarong." The smile grew. "Would you like me to show you?"

As he reached down she jerked her hand away. "I'm sure I can figure it out for myself. Thanks just the same."

"All right. I was only trying to help." As he ambled away he called over his shoulder, "As long as you're stuck lying around in the sun for a few days, you may as well get out of those awful military clothes and be comfortable."

She knew he was right. Still, she wondered how foolish she would look wrapped in a sarong, lazing on a sun-warmed beach. A tailored suit and attaché case suited her far better than this.

While Jay prepared the dinner, she slipped out of her clothes and began to wrap the piece of cloth about her. The delicate silken fabric felt soft against her skin. After nearly two weeks in sturdy khakis, the contrast felt sinfully luxurious. There was just enough cloth to cover her from hips to chest. She tied the ends of the fabric into a knot above her breasts.

Without even being aware of it, the graceful native attire caused a subtle transformation in Ann. Her previously hurried, purposeful strides were slowed by gauze-encased feet. The soft material molded itself to her firm breasts. Her hips swayed rhythmically beneath the silken fabric as she walked. Her face, drawn to the sun, lifted in an almost haughty pose. Tawny waves of hair, now dry and silky, danced about her naked shoulders.

As she walked toward the camp, Jay paused in his work to watch her. The sight of her caused him to catch his breath. And what was even more appealing was the fact that she had absolutely no idea how she looked. She was utterly guileless.

"Something smells wonderful." She gave him a dazzling smile. "I'm surprised you're such a good cook, Jay."

"I have a healthy appetite too," he replied, smiling wickedly. "For food, wine . . . women."

She ignored the insinuation. "Can I help?"

"With the dinner, or were you offering to satisfy some other hunger?"

Her cheeks and throat warmed with a sudden flush. "Don't start that again, Jay."

"I'm sorry you feel that way. I'd really like to start again, but . . . all right. Let's eat." His light dismissal confused her. With his teasing nature, he usually kept up the taunting until she lost her temper. Now what kind of game was he playing?

Ann ate heartily. Jay watched with mild amusement, remembering that when she had first arrived on the island she had been too impatient to even bother about food.

"This is wonderful." She sat beside him, leaning back against a sun-warmed rock. "It must be heavenly to grow up in such a paradise."

He nodded. "I had a marvelously carefree boyhood. Leaving here was one of the hardest things I ever had to do."

She glanced at him. "Why would you leave here?"

"I had to get an education. My father worried that I was growing up too wild and free. And I suppose I was. Even though I was exposed to a steady stream of visiting scientists and naturalists, and had the advantage of a complete library here on the island, I lacked the discipline to put the knowledge to good use." Jay shook his head, remembering. "I was thirteen when my father decided that it was time I discovered my other heritage."

"What do you mean—your other heritage?" Ann watched the blue of his eyes while he spoke. They were the same deep blue as the cloudless sky.

"My ancestors came from Scotland. My father wanted me to know something about their homeland, so he arranged for me to attend a boarding school there when I was thirteen."

Now she understood why his speech occasionally reverted to that wonderful soft burr of his ancestors. "That's so young. What did your mother say?"

Jay squinted against the sun. "She agreed. Her health was very fragile. She worried that she couldn't spend the time with my sister and me that we needed. I had grown up thinking the whole world was as carefree as my island. I think my parents were afraid I wouldn't have any concept of reality. So they shipped me halfway around the world to school. It was very hard at first." He leaned his head back and closed his eyes. "That first winter was the bleakest of my young life. I thought I'd never see the sun again. Do you know how desolate the moors can look, all cold and windswept?" Blue eyes opened wide, and he smiled at Ann's sad look. "Don't worry. I survived. Fortunately, I was allowed to spend holidays here with my family. But from the time I was thirteen, until I finished my university training, I was away more than I was here."

"Did you stay in Scotland the entire time?"

He shook his head. "After college I chose to study veterinary medicine in the United States, at Michigan State University. They have one of the finest vet schools in the country. It was there that I got the opportunity to study large herds of cattle and sheep, and learned how to manage my time wisely." He smiled, remembering. "It was also there that I discovered what snowstorms are really like. And I even learned how to ski."

"Why didn't you become a scientist like your father?"

He crossed his hands behind his head. "I spent a lot of years watching my father study birds. And one thing struck me about scientists. They observe, take notes and learn, but they never interfere with nature. That isn't their job. When my father saw a sick bird he wanted to know what caused the sickness. But I always wanted to know how to cure it."

Jay turned to Ann. "I could never just stand back and wait for nature to cure or kill. Can you understand that?"

At his passionate words, she felt a kinship with him. For one brief moment she was afraid to speak, afraid to trust her voice. She swallowed. "Yes, I understand that completely. And I think it's . . . admirable."

He stood and began clearing the remains of their

dinner. When she began to stand up he motioned for her to remain seated. "You promised to stay off your feet as much as possible, remember?"

"I feel guilty just sitting here while you work."

"Just relax and enjoy this, Ann. It isn't going to last long. As soon as your feet are healed, it's back to work for you. A lifetime of it, I suspect."

While he banked the fire Ann studied the orange globe of the sun slowly sinking beneath the crimson-tipped waves of the sea.

They sat on the sandy beach, watching an occasional sea bird skim the waters. Their shrill call was sad, lonely. Yet this isolated haven felt anything but lonely to Ann. For the first time she felt comfortable with Jay. He had opened up and told her a little about himself. It cheered her to think of the young boy growing up wild and free on this lovely island. How different their childhoods had been. Yet each had known times of isolation and loneliness; each had had to rely on his or her own strengths.

His deep voice broke into her reverie.

"Time to change those dressings before we go to sleep. Come on, I'll carry you."

He held out a hand and she stood. "I can walk."

Before she could take a step, he scooped her up into his arms and headed for the tent. His strong arms were the most wonderful haven she had ever known. She let her head drop, resting a cheek against his shoulder. She could learn to like this, even begin to depend on this man. How ironic. She had thought Jay McFarland was too laidback, too undependable to be her guide. And suddenly, it seemed the most natural thing in the world for her to be trusting him completely.

Gently he set her down on the mattress and unwrapped her feet. After fresh dressings were applied he smiled.

"Those feet look pretty good. Another day or two and I think you'll be back in business." He studied her face, allowing his gaze to linger on the fringe of lashes which dipped suddenly to shield her eyes. "Can I get you anything before I turn out the lantern?"

"No. I'm fine."

The smile deepened. "You certainly are." He pulled the blanket up and smoothed it before touching a fingertip to her cheek. "You are one fine woman, Ann Lowry."

She shivered at the intense light in his eyes. When he snapped off the light she could still see that midnight blue gaze, and it caused the heat to rush to her cheeks.

She watched his darkened figure outlined against the night sky. He stretched his arms above his head, removing his shirt. She trembled. He sat for a moment to remove his shoes. Then the mattress sagged as he drew back the blanket and climbed into bed.

The thought of lying beside him, so near, just a breath away, caused her pulse to throb in her temple. She never would have believed that she could actually share a tent and a bed with a virile man like Jay, and gradually become comfortable with the situation. Yet here they were, lying side-by-side, spending every waking and sleeping moment together—and the situation she had thought would be intolerable was actually pleasurable.

She had even found herself confiding in this man as if he were a best friend. For such an intensely private person as Ann, this was a major step in their relationship.

"Ann."

In the darkness she turned her head toward the deep voice.

"How did you happen to become a scientist? Aside from the fact that your parents were scientists, what drove you to such a difficult choice of study?"

"I suppose the first reason is that a scientist must possess an open, curious mind. I had so many questions, and my uncle had no time to answer them. So I began to lose myself in books." He heard the smile in her voice. "For a number of years, my bedroom was in his study. And because Uncle Frank would never permit me to simply read for the pleasure of reading, I had to justify the time I spent with books. So I began to read heavy, literary studies, and books that explored new ideas and new worlds."

"And that led to science?"

"I suppose. I think I've always been a scientist first, and then a person. I've always wanted to know everything. Everything."

He heard the emphasis on the last word. "And I suppose, before you knew it, learning everything took up all your time. There was no time left for the joy of learning about yourself. That can be fun, you know."

"Fun," she said almost bitterly. "No. There was no time for fun."

"And there has never been a man in your life, Ann."

She had somehow anticipated the subject, but still his

remark stung. "I suppose, just because I'm a dedicated scientist, you see me as some ageless, sexless professor."

"No, little Annie." His voice deepened. "That isn't at all the way I see you."

She shivered at his words.

"But I'm afraid that's how you see yourself." He paused. "Maybe you're just reflecting your uncle's attitude. But it's up to you to confront your sexuality. You know, it is possible to be a scientist and a woman." He heard her quick intake of breath, as if he'd shocked her.

Ann was grateful for the darkness hiding the heat flaming her cheeks. What did he know about her sexuality? What did he know about being shy, about feeling plain? It was obvious that he had always been comfortable with himself, with the way he looked, with his relationships to other people.

To him she was a source of amusement. Jay McFarland and his teasing ways. What did he know about her life, her loneliness, her yearnings?

"Ann."

She started. "What now?"

He knew by her tone that she was hurt. He hated to add to her pain, but it couldn't be helped. There was no turning back.

"Forgive this fool, but have you ever honestly expressed your feelings?"

"Oh, Jay." Wearily she turned her back on him. "Let me alone."

"Answer me, Ann. Fight with me if you want. Yell.

Scream.'' He chuckled. ''Even swear if you'd like, little missionary. But try saying exactly what you feel. It won't hurt nearly as much as you think.''

His words were greeted with a long silence.

''Come on, Ann. Open up.''

She turned, stung by his words. ''All right. Here are some honest thoughts from a very tired woman.'' He realized with a grin that she emphasized ''woman.'' ''Why don't you shave that ridiculous mess off your face?''

There was a moment of shocked silence as Ann realized that she had actually hurled—no, shouted—an insult. Her uncle would have been appalled. She had been raised to behave better than this.

''You don't like my beard?''

''You look like Bigfoot. Like some hairy monster.''

His voice rose. ''You don't like my beard?''

''I . . . I don't know. I haven't any basis for comparison. I'd like to see your face. I'd like to see the shape of your jaw. I'd like to know if you're . . . handsome.''

He roared with laughter. ''Take my word for it, there are women who think I am.''

''Oh!'' She wished she had something to throw. ''Your father said you were flamboyant. I think the word should be conceited.''

''You really don't like my beard?'' He absently stroked the shaggy growth on his chin. ''I thought it gave me character.''

''Can we drop this conversation?''

She felt him sit up in the darkness. ''We could try an experiment.''

She sat up beside him, eager to change the subject and willing to try anything scientific. "What is it?"

Too late, she detected the warmth of his mocking laughter. "You could make love with me tonight, with this beard. Then tomorrow I could shave it off, and we could make love again. Then we'll have an authentic scientific observation on which type of man is more virile—one with a beard or one without."

"Oh." She turned away. "I should have known it would be something silly."

He caught her arm. "You do have to admit you enjoyed being honest, didn't you?"

"Goodnight, Jay."

She slid beneath the covers. Slowly her lips curved in a wide smile. Yes. She had to admit. She'd enjoyed her moment of honesty. She'd enjoyed sparring with Jay. Now that she better understood his teasing nature, she felt better able to return the jibes.

On an impulse, she said, "Jay."

She felt him turn in the darkness.

"What?"

"Why haven't you ever married?"

There was a strained silence, and for a moment Ann regretted her question. Then she remembered his cutting comments about honesty and her sexuality, and renewed the attack.

"You lectured me about honesty. Now it's your turn. You're a very . . . earthy man. Why haven't you ever married?"

His tone was dangerously low. "I think we've had

enough honesty for one night. Don't push your luck, Ann.''

"Come on. I want an honest answer."

He sat up and, catching her by the arm, hauled her up beside him in the darkness.

"You've gone far enough." His breath was hot against her cheek.

"Oh, I see. You can dish it out but you can't take it. It's all right for you to demand honesty from me, but you're not prepared to return the favor."

She heard a deep sigh of resignation.

"Maybe I just don't want to be tied down with one demanding woman."

That was greeted with silence.

He sighed. "Maybe I just want a little more time to act like a barbarian. There are a lot of women out there. I need to spread myself around." He chuckled.

More silence.

He nearly groaned. "All right. This is a very isolated island, Ann. There aren't many women who would be willing to give up the excitement of the real world to spend a lifetime hidden away in the middle of the Pacific Ocean."

She could hear the sincerity in his tone. Finally he had spoken the truth. But she felt no victory in this admission. She was certain it had cost him something to say those words.

Her own voice was now subdued. "There may not be many women who could stand this isolation, but I'll bet there are some. You'll just have to keep looking."

The hand on her arm tightened its grip. He was drawing her closer. Her heartbeat quickened. By teasing him she had actually seemed to encourage this. But the truth was that she was still unable to forget their last encounter. The simmering passions she had felt—not only in Jay's urgent kisses, but in her responses—terrified her. She wasn't yet ready to deal with this unknown emotion. She was getting in way over her head, and she knew it.

"Jay."

"Shhh. Don't say a word. No more talking. I'm tired of this conversation."

His hand cupped the back of her head. His lips gently moved over hers until they parted for him.

The kiss became more urgent. He pulled her down beside him, drawing her into his embrace. The silky sarong was no barrier between them. He had to be aware of her body straining toward him. Every nerve ending, every fiber of her being yearned for him.

"Jay." She pulled away a bit, trying to explain.

"Don't say a thing, Ann. Just let it happen."

His lips pressed closer, moving over her mouth with practiced seduction.

She was infused with heat. The heat of his body. The heat of the tropics. The heat of her passion. All threatened to rob her of her will. A dangerous lethargy seemed to pervade her senses. There was no time to think. No time to argue that this could lead her to something she couldn't handle.

She moved in his arms, drawing him to her. But there was no satisfaction in the embrace. She was on fire, wanting to get closer still. Nothing would satisfy this craving for him.

His hand moved along her back, dipping to the curve of her waist, smoothing over her hip, bringing her closer to him.

She stiffened, holding back.

He raised himself up on one elbow. "I can't take any more of this, Ann. Do you know what hell you're putting me through? I can't lie beside you night after night, knowing you're there, wanting you and denying what I feel."

She pressed trembling fingers to his lips. "Don't say any more. Just let me be." There were no words to express her fear of what she had begun to feel. What she needed was time to deal with this. It was so new for her. She was afraid. Afraid she'd do the wrong thing. Afraid too that she would be hurt.

She pulled away. He didn't know. He couldn't understand what she was feeling. This man had the power to destroy her. She had never felt this kind of emotion for another man. If she gave in to these passions and he didn't return her love, it would crush her.

"I can't think, Jay."

He pulled her against the length of him, one hand stroking her hair as he murmured words of endearment against her temple.

She held herself stiffly in his arms until the frustrating tensions burst. "Don't touch me, Jay."

"Stop fighting it, Ann."

All the lessons he had been teaching her—about allowing her feelings to show, about honesty—had brought a full range of emotions to the surface. It was all too new, too raw. At last she found the strength to push herself away from him. Her heart hammered in her chest. Her breath burned in her throat.

"I said no, Jay."

He rolled away, swearing softly. A moment later she heard him push aside the covers and stand up.

"Where are you going?"

"For a walk." The words were clipped.

"It's pitch black out there."

"I'm a big boy now. I can take care of myself."

She could hear the sarcasm in his tone. The passion of a moment ago had turned to fury.

She rolled to her stomach, trying to still the tremors that still wracked her body. There was no relief for them.

Chapter Nine

Ann awoke quickly. She was instantly aware that the space beside her was empty. Jay. Had he spent the entire night walking?

She rolled to his side of the bed and felt the warm imprint of his body which lingered beneath the blanket. Sometime during the night, after she had fallen asleep, he must have returned to bed.

She sat up, then strode to the entrance of the tent. She was so intent on finding Jay that she completely forgot the gauze wrapped about her feet. Forgotten also was the daringly brief sarong, which revealed more of her than it covered.

Outside the tent, she held her hand to her forehead, shielding her eyes from the brilliant sunlight reflected off the ocean's waves. Far out, riding the foaming surf, she could see Jay.

Relief flooded through her. She started toward the shore. At the water's edge, she suddenly paused as waves washed over her feet. Chill sensations reminded her of the bandages she wore.

She took quick little steps backward, to avoid being swamped by the surf. Seeing a giant wave rolling toward her, she turned and ran for the safety of the beach. A moment later Jay's angry voice sounded behind her.

"What are you doing out here?"

She whirled. He was clad in only a thin pair of jogging shorts, which clung to his skin. Beads of water glistened in his hair and ran in tiny rivulets down his chest.

"I was looking for you. I'm afraid I forgot about my feet until it was too late. The gauze is soaked."

"Come on. I'll change the dressings."

He held out his arms to carry her, but she turned and marched ahead of him to the tent. Inside, she dropped down on the mattress and wordlessly lifted her foot for his inspection.

"Good. Very good." He examined the second foot and met her direct gaze. "They look fine. If you'd like to swim today I don't think it'll hurt. But other than that, try to stay off your feet as much as possible. I think we can return to the rain forest tomorrow."

"Thank you." She tried to imitate his noncommittal attitude. Hearing the tone of his voice only served to remind her of their last angry scene. Their tempers were growing shorter by the day, and they still had a long time to spend in each other's company.

As she strode from the tent and down to the water's

edge, Jay sat back on his heels, watching her with an angry expression.

Ann frolicked in the surf for over an hour, feeling her taut muscles relax. It was good to be active again. She had needed this physical release.

When she finally walked from the water and dropped down to let the sun dry and warm her, Jay watched from a nearby rock. His gaze skimmed the wet fabric that hugged the curves of her body like a second skin. She extended her arms above her head, stretching like a cat, then wriggled her toes contentedly.

His eyes narrowed. The transformation in her was complete. This slumbrous creature lazing in the sun bore no resemblance to the prim, overly shy scientist who had hidden her womanhood behind her dedication to her work. This woman seemed quite comfortable doing nothing more strenuous than swimming. She had emerged from the surf with unself-conscious grace, a woman completely in tune with herself and her surroundings. But her inner conflict, he knew, was still raging. The transformation of that inner person would occur more slowly.

His brow was furrowed in concentration as he slid from the rock and began jogging along the beach. Caught up in a whirlwind of changes, Ann would be extremely vulnerable now. Feeling like a beautiful woman, she would begin to experience a woman's needs and desires. For the first time in her life, perhaps, she would have to deal with making choices. Choices that up to now she hadn't even considered. Choices that could cause her pain. But choices that might also give her freedom.

He scowled and decided to jog a few more miles.

"I thought I'd surprise you by making dinner tonight for a change."

Jay stared at the fish sizzling over the fire, the taro carefully pounded into mush in a bowl. His gaze lingered a moment on her cloud of tawny hair, the bright hibiscus tucked flirtatiously behind one ear.

"Where did you get the fish?"

"The same place you always do. From the ocean." She smiled, and he noticed that her eyelashes fluttered teasingly.

"I meant, how did you manage to catch them?"

"With a net. You taught me how."

"Umm. So I did." He turned away. "I'm going for a swim to cool off first."

"I'll join you."

He gave her a steady look. "I'll only be a few minutes. I thought I'd wash my hair while I was swimming." He strode away quickly, avoiding the confusion in her eyes.

During dinner Jay was unusually quiet. Ann's attempts to engage him in conversation failed miserably and finally, in silence, they cleaned up the remains of their meal and retired to the tent for the evening.

Jay seemed engrossed in a book. Each time Ann allowed herself to glance at him, his gaze was fastened to the page as if in a trance. In exasperation she stood, making an elaborate attempt to appear tired.

The dressings had been removed from her feet. There was no need to apply ointment, and no reason she could think of for interrupting Jay's reading and getting his attention.

"I think I'll go to bed now. Goodnight, Jay."

He kept his gaze glued to the page, but he couldn't have repeated a single word written there. "Fine. Goodnight."

"Aren't you tired, Jay?"

"No."

For nearly an hour she tossed and turned, sighing audibly from time to time. Finally she sat up.

"Jay, would you mind turning out that lantern? I can't seem to get to sleep with it on."

"No problem." He snapped out the light, and she smiled in the darkness.

Straining to make out his figure, she waited to feel him climb into bed beside her. Instead, she saw him near the tent entrance.

"Aren't you coming to bed?"

"No. I think I'll walk a while."

He was gone before she could utter a word of protest. Frustrated, she pounded the pillow and wondered what was happening to her. From the beginning, she had been fighting Jay's attraction to her. Now, when she was starting to think she might like to experience what lovemaking was all about, he treated her like an untouchable.

Without ceremony they returned to the rain forest and settled back into their routine. While Jay was responsible for making and breaking camp and preparing their meals, Ann spent most of her waking day in research. Her daily journal kept her writing long into the night.

Jay made no attempt to resume a relationship, and her awkward attempts were gently rebuked. Hurt and puzzled, she drove herself to work even harder.

It was to be their last day in the rain forest. Ann's energy level was at its peak—her last chance to complete all the assignments she had mapped out for herself before returning to academic life. One last chance to breathe in the heady scents of exotic flowers that perfumed the moist air.

This place was intoxicating, a true paradise for naturalists.

Near a crystal pool, Ann knelt and took soil samples. As she worked, she thought about other scientists who would make the same journey she had. A stranger would come here next year, to work on his or her own projects. A stranger would swim in this pool, bathed in golden rays. Her heart felt heavy at the thought.

She closed her backpack and walked on, determined to continue her study up to the last possible moment.

Far behind her, Jay broke camp and followed her trail.

She tramped for nearly a mile before stopping suddenly. Her mind had been unconsciously cataloging plants as she moved through the lush foliage. Now, stunned, she stopped and retraced her steps. Nearly hidden beneath tall ferns was a species of orchid she had never before seen.

Electrified, she stooped to examine the pale bloom. Removing her notebook, she began recording the size and shape, the exact contours of its leaves and petals. Next she photographed it from every possible angle.

Jay found her seated on the floor of the forest, carefully writing in her journal. She looked up with a gleam of intense excitement glittering in her amber eyes.

"Look what I've found!"

"An orchid. Is it special?"

"I think so. I won't be certain until I've had a chance to go through all the recorded species. But I think I may have found one that has never been cataloged." She smiled suddenly. "Oh Jay. Wouldn't that be something, if I've actually found a new species of orchid?"

"Yes. I hope it's so, for your sake. Will you get to name it?"

She hadn't thought about that. "Oh, yes. Wouldn't that be fun?"

Jay knelt down beside her. "For someone who's been too busy to have much fun, you're certainly making up for lost time."

She laughed. "You're right." She took a deep breath. "Oh, why does it have to end? I think I could go right on having fun for the rest of my life."

Jay's gaze swept over her animated features. Soft hair frizzed about her cheeks and even dipped across one eyebrow. Behind her ear she had tucked a brilliant scarlet blossom. Her eyes seemed lit with an inner light. Gone forever was the prim little scientist who hid behind heavy suits and spoke in textbook terms.

He dropped his heavy pack and sat down, leaning his back against a tree. He took out a cigar from his pocket, lit it, then watched a curl of smoke drift skyward.

Her movements were quick, efficient. Changing lenses on the camera, she moved in for a closer picture.

"Do you follow up this work with study in the laboratory?"

She nodded, decided she didn't like the angle of the camera, and moved it before focusing.

"Where do you do the lab work, Ann?"

She snapped off several pictures, then changed lenses again and set the camera at another angle.

"I use the university lab. It's probably one of the best equipped labs in the country."

He watched her in silence for long minutes. "I suppose that work means a lot to you."

She moved faster, snapping off several more pictures before changing the lens.

"I suppose." Actually, she found lab work tedious. Her heart lay in field research. This was where she wanted to be. One with nature. She found the sterile environment of the laboratory stifling.

"And I suppose," he muttered, narrowing his eyes to watch a puff of smoke drift toward a sunbeam, "it would mean quite a sacrifice, for a scientist to give up the best equipped lab in the country to be stuck on a Pacific island for the rest of her life."

"Umm." Ann sat with her back to him, writing furiously, determined to record everything about this orchid before moving on. His words shattered her attention. With her pen poised above the paper, she felt tiny jolts of excitement tingling along her spine.

To spend the rest of her life on this island, with Jay, would be heaven. To know that she could repeat this trip, spend as much time as she wanted in this naturalist's paradise, would make her life complete.

To be part of his close-knit, loving family; to sit at his father's feet while he talked of his research; to join in their animated conversations around the dinner table; and most of all, to spend a lifetime with Jay. It was all she wanted.

Ann slowly closed her notebook and capped the pen. Had he been proposing, or was he just trying to find out whether or not she would be willing to live here before broaching the subject of marriage?

Marriage. A lifetime of love. How could she tell him all the things locked in her heart? With her pulse pounding in her temples she turned, a tender smile playing on her lips.

Jay was gone. Through the trees she saw his rigid back disappear into the forest. How long had she been daydreaming? How long had he waited for her reply before giving up in defeat?

Frantically, she scrambled to stuff her equipment back into her pack. Her fingers felt stiff and awkward from nervousness. At last she closed the pack and hurried in the direction he had taken.

Dinner was eaten in strained silence. Ann tried everything she could to engage Jay in conversation. It was as if he had already left her. His responses to her questions were clipped and polite.

That night, while she made her final notes in a now thick journal, he smoked and read in sullen silence.

When at last she crawled into bed, she lay there, listening to the rain, plotting a way to force Jay to talk to her. This was her last chance.

What had happened? He had gone from a carefree, teasing stranger, to a passionate man who thrilled yet frightened her, to a gentle, caring friend. But now he was none of those. Now he had become a surly, uncommunicative guide, eager to be finished with his job and her.

When at last he turned off the lantern and climbed into bed, Ann rubbed sweating palms on the flowery shirt, Jay's shirt, which she had purposely worn to bed.

She wasn't at all certain she could be a temptress, but she was determined to try. She had to make Jay aware of her feelings for him. Her future, her life, depended on tonight.

"Jay." She reached out a hand, tentatively touching his shoulder.

His skin was warm, and she deliberately kept her hand there, feeling the heat flow to her.

"Yes?" He kept his back to her.

"I want you to know how much I appreciate all you've done for me. It can't have been easy for you to let your own work go in order to accommodate me."

"I did this for my father, Ann. Long before I met you I promised him I would guide his guest through the rain forest. It had nothing to do with you personally."

She licked her lips. "But you've been very patient. I . . . thank you."

"You're welcome. Goodnight."

He shrugged off her hand and she pressed it to her mouth, holding back the sigh that threatened to escape.

"Jay."

She heard him expel his breath.

"What?"

"Would you . . ." She took a deep breath and spoke very quickly, before she lost her nerve. ". . . kiss me?"

There was a terrible silence. In the darkness she felt Jay turn toward her. When he spoke, the heat of his breath seared her temple.

"Why? Are you hoping one kiss will lead to another? Do you want to test your newfound power, to see if I'll lose control again?" His words were cruel, tinged with barely controlled fury. "Are you thinking of seducing me, Ann? Did you hope to experience the thrill of lovemaking before going back to your laboratory? Do you see it as some sort of souvenir—from a tropical paradise?"

"Oh! How can you—"

His angry words interrupted her. "You'd better face some facts, Dr. Lowry. You came into this rain forest a zealous little child-woman, devoted to science to the exclusion of all else. Now, you've discovered what it is to be a woman. You want to experience all the joys, the desires of a woman. All right, Ann. That's your right. But along with that right comes responsibility. You're not a child turned loose in a toy factory." His voice lowered dangerously. "And I'm not one of the toys."

He leaned on one elbow, and the hot, angry words washed over her, shaming her.

"Now that you're a woman, Ann, you have to accept the responsibilities of a woman. If you play, you pay. And the chances of getting hurt are much greater." His voice dropped to nearly a whisper. "Would you still like to seduce me, doctor?"

Covering her face with her hands, she turned toward the wall of the tent, too ashamed to even speak.

Long moments later, she heard Jay moving about in the darkness. Then he was gone into the night.

Ann followed Jay's steady strides through the forest. He had become a stranger. They had breakfasted in silence. After breaking camp they had begun the long trek back to their original point of entrance. Jay's directions were given in monosyllables. He never once looked back to see if she was able to keep up.

She was grateful when at last they passed through the veil of mist and saw the jeep.

Chapter Ten

As the dusty jeep drew near the McFarland house Jay turned to Ann.

"Company," he said, pointing to the vehicle parked near the front porch. "Probably Janet and Colin. It's like them to keep a close eye on Dad while I'm gone."

Before he even had time to turn off the ignition the sound of Laela's shrill voice reached them. After calling to everyone in the house she hurled herself into Jay's arms.

"Doc Jamie. I've missed you."

"I missed you too, Shrimp. Every once in a while I had to carry Ann around, just to stay in shape. Keeping up with your studies?"

She laughed at his silly joke. "Of course. You said I can be a vet when I learn as much as you." She wrapped her arms about his neck and hugged him fiercely.

By the time he set her down his sister and her husband were walking down the front steps.

"Will you look at him," Janet said to Colin. "If possible, he looks even more primitive than when he left. Ann, I thought you were going to civilize this brother of mine."

She glanced at Ann, and her mouth dropped slightly open. This couldn't be the perfectly turned-out little scientist she had met only a month ago. Her quick inspection took in the cloud of blond hair and glowing skin, kissed by the sun. Even a few dirty smudges couldn't mar the beauty of the woman standing before her.

"Ann." Colin quickly covered up his wife's surprise by taking Ann's hand in his. "How was your month?"

"It was fine, Colin. I think I may have even managed to locate an uncataloged species of orchid. How is Dr. McFarland?"

"Just fine." Colin lifted her pack from the jeep and slapped Jay on the back. "Here. Give me your pack too. Your dad's dying to see you."

Jay nodded and climbed the steps beside Ann. Behind them Janet lifted an eyebrow in surprise. "Would you have believed this?"

He grinned at the look on her face. "It looks like our Dr. Lowry decided to join your rascal of a brother in his primitive lifestyle. And I must say, on her it looks good."

Janet playfully smacked his shoulder. "Just leave the looking to Jamie." She took one of the packs from his arms. "Come on. Let's hear all about life in the forest primeval."

Dr. McFarland was delighted to welcome his son. And if he found Ann's appearance a surprise, he covered it well.

"My dear. I can't wait to hear all about your field trip. Are you satisfied with your accomplishments?"

She nodded. "Your rain forest was everything I had hoped, Dr. McFarland."

"Good. I'm so happy for you." He turned to his son, who stood quietly by the desk. "And you, Jamie lad. Any problems?"

Jay shook his head. "None, Dad. It went well." He avoided looking at Ann while he wiped his palms along his soiled cut-offs. "Now, if you don't mind, I think we could both use a shower and rest before dinner. Then we'll talk."

"Of course. Mala has planned a big dinner for tonight. To be topped off, of course, by your favorite dessert—chocolate ice cream."

Ian was surprised at Jay's lack of enthusiasm. "That's fine, Dad. I'll see you in a little while."

As Ann and Jay walked from the room, Ian studied them thoughtfully.

While they made their way upstairs, Laela hung on Jay's arm, trying to tell him in five minutes everything that had happened for the past month. At Ann's door he paused for a moment, as if about to speak, then, apparently thinking better of it, continued down the hall with Laela still clutching his arm.

In her room, Ann stared at the luxurious appointments and wondered what had happened to her. Instead of feeling thrilled at the thought of a comfortable bed and soothing bath she found herself wishing she could go back to the tent and the mattress she had shared with Jay.

She caught sight of herself in the mirror and stared in shocked surprise. The woman staring back at her was a stranger. She touched a hand to the mane of hair. It looked wild and tangled. She reached a tentative finger-tip to the tanned cheek. There was a glow about her that she had never seen before. Her gaze traveled down the slender body barely covered by her cut-off shorts and shirt. She felt a flush begin at her throat and slowly burn across her cheeks. So this was what Jay had seen.

She filled the tub and stripped off her clothes. For a long time she simply laid her head back against the tub, feeling the warmth soothe her tired muscles. Finally she shampooed her hair, then lathered her body with fragrant soap. Wrapped in a robe, feeling exhausted beyond words, she slipped between scented sheets and slept.

A soft knock on her door awakened her.

"Yes? Come in."

Janet poked her head in. "Did I wake you, Ann?"

"Umm." She struggled to clear her mind. "How long have I been sleeping?"

"Nearly two hours. Mala said dinner will be ready in a little while. I wanted to catch you before you dressed." She stepped inside and Ann realized Janet was holding something behind her back.

Ann sat up, tossing her hair behind her shoulder. "What's that?"

Janet grinned. "You admired my dress, and I decided to look for something similar in Honolulu for you. Here."

She handed Ann a box. Nestled in layers of tissue paper was the most beautiful dress Ann had ever seen. She jumped out of bed and held it up in front of her.

"Oh Janet. I don't know what to say. It's fabulous."

"I'm glad you approve. I hope it fits."

Ann behaved in a completely uncharacteristic manner. Without any hesitation or embarrassment, she untied her robe and stepped into the dress.

Janet zipped and snapped, then stepped back to inspect the result.

The fabric was delicate swirls of lavenders and pinks. The dress, tied with lavender ribbons over each shoulder, was cut low at the fitted bodice, then fell in a drift of pure silk nearly to her ankles.

"Oh, Ann, it's perfect." Janet removed the tissue and showed the second surprise beneath. "I hope these are your size."

She held up a pair of palest lavender sandals, with spiky heels and lavender ribbons that twined about the ankles.

Ann gave a delighted sigh, then sat on the edge of the bed and tried them on. They fit as if made for her.

She gave Janet a hug. "I feel like Cinderella. Oh, Janet, what a wonderful surprise."

She twirled in front of the full-length mirror, laughing

in delight. Janet was reminded of Laela. This young woman had the same sense of childlike wonder.

"I'll see you downstairs in a little while, Ann."

"Janet."

She turned in the doorway.

"Thank you."

She nodded, then hurried out.

Ann followed the sound of voices to the brick-paved patio, where Jay and his father were talking quietly. She paused in the doorway and Jay's head came up sharply, like a hound scenting its prey.

He turned, and she felt his gaze burn slowly over her.

"Ann, my dear. Come in."

Ian stood, leaning heavily on his cane, and indicated the seat next to him.

"Jamie, why don't you fix Ann a drink."

Jay continued to stare at her and Ann, feeling suddenly self-conscious in her glamorous attire, was grateful to sit beside the elderly man.

"Jamie was just telling me that in his mail was a letter informing him that another of his papers on veterinary medicine has been published."

Ann glanced at Jay's broad back as he fixed her drink at the bar.

"That's wonderful. What's it about?"

He turned. "My specialty is the prevention of tropical diseases, especially through selective breeding. The vast cattle and sheep herds here on the island offer a perfect opportunity to put my theories into practice."

"It must take up a lot of your time."

"That's something I have in abundance," he muttered. As he handed Ann a drink Jay's hand lingered a moment on hers. "That's a new dress, isn't it?"

She flushed. "Yes. Janet bought it as a surprise."

"It's perfect on you. You look beautiful."

She glanced down, her throat so tight her voice seemed caught in it. "Thank you."

In a few minutes Janet and Colin joined them, and the talk drifted to Jay's latest paper and then to the rain forest and the study Ann had conducted.

At Mala's announcement they moved to the dining room. It was obvious that Mala had gone to great pains to make this meal special. Along with aged prime beef, she had prepared finnan haddie, a Scottish specialty of smoked haddock, which she claimed was Jay's favorite. There was a mouth-watering casserole of potatoes and vegetables, sweetened with island pineapple. Bread still warm from the oven nestled in a basket.

As lovely as it was, Ann found she had little appetite for all the food she had missed for the past month.

Jay, whose appetite was famous, seemed equally disinterested. While Mala hovered, clucking like a mother hen, Jay forced himself to eat. But when, at the end of the meal, he refused a second helping of chocolate ice cream, she looked worried.

"Jamie, are you coming down with something?"

He lifted one eyebrow and sent her a scathing look. "I'm fine, Mala. And the meal was perfect. I'm just not accustomed to this much food. Give me a few days."

She sniffed her disapproval and scuffled from the room, much to the amusement of Janet and Colin.

After dinner, the conversation drifted and swirled about her, and Ann found herself barely able to concentrate. She stole a glance at Jay's face. He was staring at her, but the frown that furrowed his brow gave him a forbidding appearance.

"What do you think, Ann?"

She tore her gaze from Jay and forced her thoughts back to the others. It was torture, being in the same room with him and unable to say what needed to be said. She would be leaving in the morning. There was so little time. And she had to make him understand that she wanted to be here with him. If only he would ask her again. If only . . .

". . . and do you know what he said, Ann?"

She smiled too brightly. "What?"

As the voices droned on she watched Jay walk across the room. He bent to whisper to his father, then bid them all goodnight.

She was stunned. Jay was going to bed. And nothing had been resolved. Everything had been left unsaid.

Ann woke at dawn and forced herself to pack. After a hurried bath she slipped on the prim navy suit she had arrived in and studied herself in the mirror. She felt uncomfortable in the stiff clothes and proper shoes. Already, she realized with a shock, the woman she had become was more familiar to her than the person she had been just a short month ago.

Brushing her hair furiously, she pulled it back in a knot at her nape. She frowned. It was too severe. Wielding the brush with quick, angry motions, she decided to leave her hair soft and loose.

With a last glance around the lovely suite of rooms, Ann made her way downstairs.

"Good morning, my dear." Ian stood as she entered. "All packed?"

She forced a bright smile. "Yes."

Janet and Colin were already dressed and enjoying coffee. Their luggage lay in the foyer.

"We're flying out with you this morning, Ann," Janet informed her. "And if there's time I thought we could shop or at least have lunch together before you catch your connection to the mainland."

Ann nodded, but her thoughts were on Jay. Scanning the room, she realized he hadn't yet come downstairs.

Mala shuffled in carrying a tray of toast and eggs. Placing the steaming plates before them, she huffed, "Jamie didn't even have time to eat a thing, and already he's gone to check on some cow. Dr. McFarland, that boy's going to make himself sick."

Ann's heart plummeted. Jay had left, without a word.

"Oh, and little doctor, Jamie told me to tell you that he wishes you all the best with your research. He said he hopes you have a good trip."

"Thank you." She glanced down quickly, fighting the sting of tears.

Janet exchanged a glance with her husband. "Well, Ann," she said cheerfully, "I think living in the wild agrees with you. You've certainly blossomed. Tell me, did you and Jamie manage to get along without too many arguments?''

Ann swallowed. "Oh, we had our share."

"Good for you." Colin smiled gently at her. "There's nothing Jay likes better than a good fight."

"If you'll excuse me." Ann pushed her chair back and stood quickly. "I'm really not hungry. And I'd like to check the room once more, to be certain I've packed everything."

As she hurried from the dining room, three pair of eyes watched in silence.

"You sit up here beside me, Dr. Lowry. You can be my copilot," Moi said cheerfully.

Janet and Colin sat behind them in the cramped passenger section of the tiny interisland plane that had delivered Ann just one month before.

As they lifted off the runway, Ann peered out the window, unable to tear her gaze from the lovely green landscape below.

"I hope our wilderness wasn't too harsh, Ann," Janet said, breaking into her thoughts.

Ann shook her head. "No. It was a gentle wilderness."

"And I hope my brother wasn't too much of a barbarian."

Ann's head moved slightly. Her voice was barely more than a whisper. "No. He was a . . . gentle barbarian."

Janet gave her husband a worried look. He shrugged and squeezed her hand.

Ann turned her head, watching the little island until it was out of sight. The others in the plane chatted quietly. She remained silent, lost in thought.

A lone figure stood at the edge of the herd of cattle. With a hand shielding his eyes from the sun, he watched the silver plane slowly circle the island before lifting heavenward.

She was tugging at his heart. That prim and proper little missionary had changed everything. He wished he had never met her.

He stared until the glint of silver disappeared on the horizon. Then he turned away, cursing himself for his stubborn Scottish pride.

"You have two hours before you catch your flight home, Ann. Which will it be—shopping or lunch?"

Ann smiled gently at Janet's attempts to cheer her. "I just couldn't handle shopping right now. How about lunch?"

"Fine," Colin interrupted. "The two of you have a good time. As for me, I'm heading to the nearest phone to take down the million and one messages that will be waiting for us."

Janet chuckled as he walked away. "It will take us a week to catch up on the work that probably piled up. But Colin is so understanding about my worries over my father."

She and Ann walked to the airport dining room and settled into a booth. After giving their order to a waitress, Janet asked, "Are you eager to get home?"

Ann seemed to think about the question for a long moment before answering. "I'm not at all sure I am. I think I fell in love with your island, Janet."

Janet smiled gently. "With my island? Or my brother?"

Ann brushed a hand across her eyes, as if trying to banish a pain. "Am I that transparent?"

"You and Jay both."

Ann stared at her a moment, puzzled. "Jay?"

"Oh, Ann. It's so obvious. That poor man is so crazy in love he's miserable. What did you do to him?"

"You have it all wrong, Janet. Jay is just angry with me. It has nothing to do with love. In fact, I'm not sure he can even stand the sight of me."

Janet sipped her iced tea and wondered what had happened between these two very different but strong-willed people.

"Janet, how did you know you loved Colin enough to want to marry him?"

Janet's thoughts turned inward, remembering the terrible uncertainties of her youthful love. "I think I suddenly realized that losing him would create a terrible void in my life. No achievement, no success would ever mean a thing if I couldn't share it with Colin. He had taken over my life."

Ann was silent for long moments. Then she met Janet's look. "Would you mind hearing something?"

She shook her head. "I think you need to talk about it, Ann."

Where to begin? Ann took a deep breath. "Jay . . . was very kind to me, at a time when I needed some kindness. And slowly, I began to realize how much he meant to me." She smiled gently, remembering. "He taught me how to laugh at his silly teasing, and how to cry and how to be honest about my feelings. But when I tried to . . ." She flushed, realizing how much of herself she was giving away by this admission. ". . . show him how I felt, he rejected me." She bit her lip to keep it from trembling. "He was very cruel. But I realize now that everything he said was the truth. And I needed to hear it." She looked up to see Janet studying her intently. "And then, on our last day in the rain forest, he asked me if I'd be willing to give up my research in the lab to stay on his island."

Her eyes clouded with the pain of that memory. "Janet, Jay wasn't asking me to give up anything. I'd be getting so much more than I could ever give. But before I could respond he had just walked away. And now he won't talk to me at all. I've lost him."

Janet watched the play of emotions on Ann's face. Her heart ached for this vulnerable young woman as well as for her proud brother. She wondered if she had the right to betray a confidence.

She took a deep breath. "Ann, years ago my brother asked a classmate of mine to marry him and live with him on our island." Janet met Ann's direct gaze. "He was very young and, at the time, very much in love.

She . . . refused. She had just invested a good many years in her medical studies. She had a chance to join an already established practice in San Francisco. It was too much to give up." She shrugged. "Or maybe the love just wasn't strong enough. For whatever reason, she rejected him."

"And now he thinks I've rejected him as well." Ann's voice grew angry. "But that isn't fair. It isn't my fault that he was refused before. What does that have to do with me?"

"Just this. Don't think you're the only one who is afraid of rejection. Even big strong men like my brother feel pain. Love can be a devastating thing, if it isn't returned." She paused a moment, then brightened. "You haven't lost him yet. Why don't you go to him? Just declare your love and tell him exactly how you feel."

Ann shook her head sadly. "I couldn't bear the humiliation if Jay refused my love." Deep in thought, she poured cream in her coffee and stared at the swirls. "I'm going back to Boston. I need to put some distance between us."

Janet started to say something, when the boarding announcement interrupted their conversation. Neither of them had eaten a thing.

Before boarding the plane Ann hugged Janet tightly. "Please, Janet, don't tell Jay what we talked about. It's so personal. Promise me you'll keep my confidence."

"All right. But I think you're wrong to leave. It isn't fair to either of you not to talk this out." She pressed the other woman's hand. "I wish you luck, Ann. I hope you know what you're doing."

As the jumbo jet climbed high over the blue Pacific, Ann turned her face into a pillow, trying to shut out all thought of the red-bearded giant who had taught her to love and then had broken her heart. But something Janet had said kept breaking through her thoughts, taunting her.

In the rain forest, Jay had patiently led her to a deeper understanding of herself. And although his cruel words still lashed her, she had needed to hear them. If she were truly a woman, with a woman's needs and desires, then she also had to be prepared to pay the price of loving.

Wasn't a man, from his earliest teens, when he began the dating ritual, preparing himself for the trauma of rejection? Each time he asked a young woman for a date he was putting his emotions on the line. A woman had the power to damage a man's self-esteem. What an awesome weapon she wielded. Yet in order to achieve any success, she had to be willing to put it all on the line as well. So why not put it all on the line for love?

Ann pressed a feverish forehead to the cool window-pane of the plane and peered far below. Already, the plan that was taking shape in her mind frightened her. What if she took a leave of absence from her job, disposed of her little house near the campus and followed her heart? Was she willing to take the consequences if Jay rejected her?

By the time the snowy landscape of Boston's Logan Airport glistened far below, Ann had waged a terrible battle within herself and had made her decision. She would gamble everything for love. And by doing so, she would give Jay the power to destroy her.

The radio was calling it the worst snowstorm of the winter. Ann set a crate of books in the hallway and decided to shovel the driveway one more time.

On the kitchen table, her airline ticket lay beside the telephone. She had just been informed that there would be no more flights out today. The runways had just closed.

She tucked her hair beneath a wool cap and zipped her ski jacket. Donning bright red mittens, she grabbed up the snow shovel, went outside and began furiously scraping the heavy snow in an effort to work off her frustration.

Heavy white flakes continued to cover the driveway. The thick blanket of snow muffled all sound. Even the distant noise of snarled traffic was muted.

Her memories of a red-bearded giant in a distant tropical paradise were so strong, she had begun to see and hear him in every passing stranger. Even now, here in this blinding snowstorm, she was imagining him here with her. The tall figure approaching her sent tingles rippling through her veins. She turned away, determined not to embarrass herself by staring at strangers.

She was so startled by the deep voice behind her that she dropped the shovel.

"I just remembered how much I hate snow."

Ann whirled. A giant, garbed in heavy parka and

boots, stood with his hands on his hips, regarding her with a frown.

"Jay!"

The look on his face was unreadable. For what seemed like forever, he simply stared at her, as if afraid to reach out and touch what appeared to be a fragile apparition. Then, with an angry, jerking motion, he picked up the shovel and took her hand, picking his way gingerly through the mounds of snow toward her door.

Inside, the steamy heat was a shocking contrast to the frigid air.

Her heart was doing crazy things inside her chest. It was so hard to breathe, she found herself taking great gulps of air. Needing to do something, anything, she pulled off the cap and let her thick tawny hair spill about her shoulders and cheeks. She saw his eyes narrow perceptibly.

For long moments he stared at her as if transfixed. Finally he tore his gaze away and stared around the tidy kitchen, then suddenly noticed the crates in the hallway.

"I just came from the university. They told me you've taken a leave of absence."

She nodded, wishing she had the courage to reach out a hand to his face. "You . . . shaved your beard."

"I do that now and then. What do you think?"

She shook her head. "You're . . . very nice-looking. Good firm jaw, like your father's. And your mouth . . ."

He smiled for the first time, and her heartbeat accelerated. "Would you care to examine my teeth? I have very good teeth."

She laughed, then pulled her thoughts together. "You were saying you came from the university. What are you doing here in Boston?"

He unbuttoned his heavy parka and tossed it over a kitchen chair. "I suppose I could say I'm just passing through." He smiled wryly. "Would you believe me?"

She shook her head, unwilling to trust her voice.

He was even taller than she remembered. And his shoulders, beneath the plaid shirt, seemed broader. His eyes were the same deep blue, and his smile was that same wonderful smile she would always be able to see, even in her dreams.

"Why did you leave the university, Ann?"

She swallowed. "I need to get away from academic life for a while."

"Where are you going?" He nodded toward the crates of books, and she followed the direction of his gaze.

"I've decided to start a new life."

She heard the sudden intake of breath, and saw the sudden look of pain that crossed his face before he composed himself.

"Would you like some coffee?" She turned away, needing to be busy. This was going to be awkward.

"No. I didn't come all this way to drink coffee. We have to talk."

"All right. But before you start, I have a few things to say."

She turned to face him.

"Not until you hear me out." There was no denying the urgency in his tone. They stared at each other across the tiny kitchen, neither willing to give in to the other.

"This time, Ann, you're going to just listen. No arguments until I've finished."

He was glowering at her and she lowered her eyes, waiting for the expected explosion of temper.

"My father misses you. He's . . . very lonely."

She stared at him in surprise. This wasn't at all what she had expected to hear.

"Your father?"

"Yes." He cleared his throat. "He misses your rapt attention when he's talking about his life's work. He misses your bright mind and your thoughtful questions. His life seems even lonelier since you left."

The smallest hint of a smile hovered about her lips.

"You've come all this way on behalf of your father. How very devoted of you."

He grinned, and her heart nearly turned over at the sight of that lazy smile. "I've always been a thoughtful son."

"Hmm. Yes, so I've noticed. Now, about the son. Does he miss me as well?"

"Shh." He touched a fingertip to her lips, and she lifted startled eyes to his.

"Dr. Lowry, you've ruined my paradise. When you left you took all the sunshine with you. Please come back and make it right."

She moved her lips gently against his fingers, feeling the fluttering deep inside. "Jay, you've managed to change all my thinking. You taught me to cry, to laugh at your teasing, to let my hair down."

He reached a hand to the tawny waves that spilled about her shoulders.

"And now, I've decided to clutter up my simple, orderly life, Jay. That's why I'm packing. I'm going to take some risks. The first step was leaving the university. The second was putting this house in the hands of a real estate agent. But the most important is this." She held up the airline ticket.

He studied it in silence, then stared at her with a puzzled expression. "Hawaii? I don't understand."

"I was supposed to leave tonight for San Francisco. Tomorrow I would have been at Kalai." She smiled as she realized something. "And if fate hadn't stepped in, we would have missed each other. Jay, quite simply, I was coming to tell you that I can't live without you. The missionary has been converted by the sinner."

He looked thunderstruck. "You were really coming to me?"

She nodded. "Heart in hand. To beg, if necessary."

He caught her shoulders in a grip so painful it startled her. "I came here for the same reason. And I was willing to grovel if I had to."

His hands cupped her face and his features became tender. "Little Annie, I've never been so lonely or so miserable in my life. Oh God, how I've missed you."

She raised herself on tiptoe to meet his lips. His arms came around her, pinning her against the length of him. The kiss between them started out as softly as the fall of a snowflake. Suddenly it flamed, hot and hungry, with all the love and passion so long denied.

When at last he lifted his mouth from hers, he scooped her into his arms and carried her to the living room.

Glancing around, he saw only one chair. The rest of the room was bare.

As he deposited her in the chair, he bent over her, keeping his lips just above hers.

"Why is this room bare?"

"I had a furniture sale. I told you, I was leaving this life behind for good. There was to be no turning back."

He groaned. "There's no couch, and two can't fit in this chair. Did you sell your bed too?"

She laughed at the devilish gleam in his eyes.

"No. It's upstairs."

He gave a sigh of relief. "Did you know that on my island, the natives need only say three times, 'I marry you,' and they're considered legally married?"

She nearly choked. "Jay! That's a bald lie."

He swore. "I forgot. A walking encyclopedia like you would know the truth." He shrugged. "Well, I tried. I suppose this means we have to be married in the traditional way?"

"Absolutely. I insist."

"All right." He knelt before her and pressed his lips into the palm of her hand. "Ann, I realize I like to tease and be silly. But this is deadly serious."

She touched his bowed head, and he met her direct gaze.

"I started out wanting to discover the woman beneath the scientist. At first it was a game. Then, of course, I discovered passion, and simply wanted to satisfy it. But once I realized just how much you meant to me, I knew I could never take advantage of you. I wanted it all. Your friendship, your passion, your love. Please say you'll marry me."

She nodded. "I will. Oh Jay, I've never been so sure of anything in my life as I am of this love I have for you. I was willing to leave behind everything I've ever had—all I've worked for—to take a chance on you." A sly smile tugged at the corners of her mouth. "But there is one thing you'll have to agree to first."

He looked grave, wondering what he would have to do.

"I simply will not tolerate chocolate ice cream for breakfast."

He burst out laughing. "Even if we pour it over wheat germ?"

She thought about it for a moment, then nodded. "I may consider that. After all, it would be nutritious as well as tasty." At his knowing smile she added, "Well, you did say some things should be enjoyed just for the pleasure they bring."

"Speaking of pleasure." He glanced at the frosted windowpane, and she recognized the glint of humor in those blue eyes. "The weather report is calling this a monster snowstorm. They said it may last for days. We're going to be trapped here—all alone."

"Then we'll just have to find something to occupy ourselves." Ann brightened. "I know. There's this experiment I've been dying to try."

Jay groaned. "Always the scientist. Can't you ever get away from research?"

She grinned conspiratorially. "I think you'll enjoy this one. It was suggested to me once that I ought to determine which sort of man is more virile—one clean-shaven, or one with a shaggy beard.''

He threw back his head in a roar of laughter at her uncharacteristic joke. ''Why, Dr. Lowry. You know I'm always willing to donate my body to science.''

''Ah, but this experiment may go on for days, weeks. Why it may even take years to conclude.''

''I'll be brave. After all, this is in the interest of science.''

He buried his lips in a tangle of hair and drew her up into his arms. ''How would you like to spend your honeymoon in a tropical rain forest, doctor?''

She snuggled into his arms as if she had always belonged there. Her fingertips brushed his neatly trimmed hair, then roamed over his smooth cheek and firm jaw. ''Umm. Yes, I think I'd like to go back and see that barbarian I fell in love with.''

''You won, little Annie,'' he murmured against her temple. ''My prim little missionary managed to convert this sinner.''

''Or has the sinner won over the missionary?''

Her fingers fumbled with the buttons of his shirt.

He smiled and drew her closer into his arms. She could feel the wild racing of his pulse.

As his lips nuzzled the sensitive hollow of her throat, something tightened deep inside her. A flame raced along her spine, heating her flesh.

Feeling her response, he lifted her in his arms and headed for the stairs.

Against her temple he murmured, ''We've both won, little Annie. A treasure. A lifetime of love.''

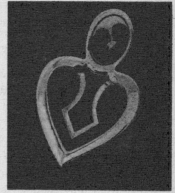

Silhouette Romance

IT'S YOUR OWN SPECIAL TIME
Contemporary romances for today's women.
Each month, six very special love stories will be yours
from SILHOUETTE.

$1.75 each

☐ 100 Stanford	☐ 128 Hampson	☐ 157 Vitek	☐ 185 Hampson
☐ 101 Hardy	☐ 129 Converse	☐ 158 Reynolds	☐ 186 Howard
☐ 102 Hastings	☐ 130 Hardy	☐ 159 Tracy	☐ 187 Scott
☐ 103 Cork	☐ 131 Stanford	☐ 160 Hampson	☐ 188 Cork
☐ 104 Vitek	☐ 132 Wisdom	☐ 161 Trent	☐ 189 Stephens
☐ 105 Eden	☐ 133 Rowe	☐ 162 Ashby	☐ 190 Hampson
☐ 106 Dailey	☐ 134 Charles	☐ 163 Roberts	☐ 191 Browning
☐ 107 Bright	☐ 135 Logan	☐ 164 Browning	☐ 192 John
☐ 108 Hampson	☐ 136 Hampson	☐ 165 Young	☐ 193 Trent
☐ 109 Vernon	☐ 137 Hunter	☐ 166 Wisdom	☐ 194 Barry
☐ 110 Trent	☐ 138 Wilson	☐ 167 Hunter	☐ 195 Dailey
☐ 111 South	☐ 139 Vitek	☐ 168 Carr	☐ 196 Hampson
☐ 112 Stanford	☐ 140 Erskine	☐ 169 Scott	☐ 197 Summers
☐ 113 Browning	☐ 142 Browning	☐ 170 Ripy	☐ 198 Hunter
☐ 114 Michaels	☐ 143 Roberts	☐ 171 Hill	☐ 199 Roberts
☐ 115 John	☐ 144 Goforth	☐ 172 Browning	☐ 200 Lloyd
☐ 116 Lindley	☐ 145 Hope	☐ 173 Camp	☐ 201 Starr
☐ 117 Scott	☐ 146 Michaels	☐ 174 Sinclair	☐ 202 Hampson
☐ 118 Dailey	☐ 147 Hampson	☐ 175 Jarrett	☐ 203 Browning
☐ 119 Hampson	☐ 148 Cork	☐ 176 Vitek	☐ 204 Carroll
☐ 120 Carroll	☐ 149 Saunders	☐ 177 Dailey	☐ 205 Maxam
☐ 121 Langan	☐ 150 Major	☐ 178 Hampson	☐ 206 Manning
☐ 122 Scofield	☐ 151 Hampson	☐ 179 Beckman	☐ 207 Windham
☐ 123 Sinclair	☐ 152 Halston	☐ 180 Roberts	☐ 208 Halston
☐ 124 Beckman	☐ 153 Dailey	☐ 181 Terrill	☐ 209 LaDame
☐ 125 Bright	☐ 154 Beckman	☐ 182 Clay	☐ 210 Eden
☐ 126 St. George	☐ 155 Hampson	☐ 183 Stanley	☐ 211 Walters
☐ 127 Roberts	☐ 156 Sawyer	☐ 184 Hardy	☐ 212 Young

$1.95 each

☐ 213 Dailey	☐ 217 Vitek	☐ 221 Browning	☐ 225 St. George
☐ 214 Hampson	☐ 218 Hunter	☐ 222 Carroll	☐ 226 Hampson
☐ 215 Roberts	☐ 219 Cork	☐ 223 Summers	☐ 227 Beckman
☐ 216 Saunders	☐ 220 Hampson	☐ 224 Langan	☐ 228 King

Silhouette Romance

$1.95 each

☐ 229 Thornton	☐ 253 James	☐ 277 Wilson	☐ 301 Palmer
☐ 230 Stevens	☐ 254 Palmer	☐ 278 Hunter	☐ 302 Smith
☐ 231 Dailey	☐ 255 Smith	☐ 279 Ashby	☐ 303 Langan
☐ 232 Hampson	☐ 256 Hampson	☐ 280 Roberts	☐ 304 Cork
☐ 233 Vernon	☐ 257 Hunter	☐ 281 Lovan	☐ 305 Browning
☐ 234 Smith	☐ 258 Ashby	☐ 282 Halldorson	☐ 306 Gordon
☐ 235 James	☐ 259 English	☐ 283 Payne	☐ 307 Wildman
☐ 236 Maxam	☐ 260 Martin	☐ 284 Young	☐ 308 Young
☐ 237 Wilson	☐ 261 Saunders	☐ 285 Gray	☐ 309 Hardy
☐ 238 Cork	☐ 262 John	☐ 286 Cork	☐ 310 Hunter
☐ 239 McKay	☐ 263 Wilson	☐ 287 Joyce	☐ 311 Gray
☐ 240 Hunter	☐ 264 Vine	☐ 288 Smith	☐ 312 Vernon
☐ 241 Wisdom	☐ 265 Adams	☐ 289 Saunders	☐ 313 Rainville
☐ 242 Brooke	☐ 266 Trent	☐ 290 Hunter	☐ 314 Palmer
☐ 243 Saunders	☐ 267 Chase	☐ 291 McKay	☐ 315 Smith
☐ 244 Sinclair	☐ 268 Hunter	☐ 292 Browning	☐ 316 Macomber
☐ 245 Trent	☐ 269 Smith	☐ 293 Morgan	☐ 317 Langan
☐ 246 Carroll	☐ 270 Camp	☐ 294 Cockcroft	☐ 318 Herrington
☐ 247 Halldorson	☐ 271 Allison	☐ 295 Vernon	☐ 319 Lloyd
☐ 248 St. George	☐ 272 Forrest	☐ 296 Paige	☐ 320 Brooke
☐ 249 Scofield	☐ 273 Beckman	☐ 297 Young	☐ 321 Glenn
☐ 250 Hampson	☐ 274 Roberts	☐ 298 Hunter	
☐ 251 Wilson	☐ 275 Browning	☐ 299 Roberts	
☐ 252 Roberts	☐ 276 Vernon	☐ 300 Stephens	

SILHOUETTE BOOKS, Department SB/1
1230 Avenue of the Americas
New York, NY 10020

Please send me the books I have checked above. I am enclosing $_____
(please add 75¢ to cover postage and handling. NYS and NYC residents please
add appropriate sales tax). Send check or money order—no cash or C.O.D.'s
please. Allow six weeks for delivery.

NAME _____

ADDRESS _____

CITY _____ STATE/ZIP _____